THE BITTER MOMENT OF TRUTH

At the end of every bullfight there comes the moment of truth, when the bullfighter must fell the bull cleanly, with dignity, honor and pride. If he does not, then all that has gone before does not matter.

But for Manuel Ortega, Spain's greatest bullfighter, there was another moment of truth. His fight was in the bedroom, not the bullring. His enemy was not the bull but the beautiful daughter of a Spanish duke.

She was his for the asking, but Manuel Ortega did not ask. What he wanted he took. Only—after it was over he knew that she had won. He would keep coming back for what she had to give until she had drained him of everything that made him a man.

MOMENT OF TRUTH

Arnold Rodin

MB

A MACFADDEN-BARTELL BOOK

THIS IS THE COMPLETE TEXT
OF THE ORIGINAL EDITION

A MACFADDEN BOOK........1969

Macfadden-Bartell Corporation
A subsidiary of Bartell Media Corporation
205 East 42nd Street, New York, New York 10017

I.

THE BEGINNING

Chapter One

The right horn was red. It was red all along its length,
from the tip all the way, following the wide curve and
back to where it grew out of the bull's black skull. The
picador had fallen between the horse and the bull and the
horn had found him as he lay on the ground. Now they
were carrying the picador from the ring and a low buzz of
anticipation came from the huge crowd as the matador
cited the bull with the wet horn.

The youth sitting in his shirt sleeves in the hot Madrid
sun high up in the stands did not buzz with the crowd. His
eyes, which were black and very bright and intense were
fixed on the scene in the bull ring. His name was Manuel
Ortega, and his friends, the few he had, called him
Manolo. This was the second bull and he had noticed
something interesting with the first bull.

As the matador passed the bull with a swirl of the
rose-colored cape the crowd roared *Olé* in time with his
movements, the *O* long and drawn out, beginning as the
matador started his pass with the cape, and the *lé,* more
staccato and crescendo, punctuating the maneuver. Four
times the matador passed the black bull, alternating from
left to right, but Manuel did not join in the *Olés*. He was
waiting for the next charge and for the next matador to
take the bull.

He was a dark, thin-faced youth not yet twenty-one,
and when he was seated as he was, bent toward the ring, it
was not apparent that he was also tall, lithe, thin-hipped,
and muscular. The black eyes, the straight black hair, and
the thin face gave him an appearance of gauntness that was
not true. He had a straight sharp nose, wide thin lips, and
a narrow pointed chin. In the sun, where he was sitting, it
was very hot and sweat running down his back made the
white shirt stick to him. Manuel's mind was on the fight,

but narrowed to one aspect of it, because it was this that had led him to spend almost his last money to buy one of the cheapest seats in the arena.

It will show with this bull, he was thinking. He wanted it to show very badly; otherwise it all would have been a waste and he would have to do it all over again and he could not wait for that. The goring of the picador was something he would not actually have hoped for, but he thought it a lucky thing and a sign that his plan would work out as he hoped.

The bull charged at the horse without hesitation and the new picador leaned over in his saddle and shot the steel-tipped lance into the swollen hump of muscle in the bull's neck, the bull insisting on the charge, seeking the horse with his horn, and the picador holding him with the lance, pivoting the horse on his hind legs and not releasing his hold on the bull till he had swung clear of the horns. The bull shot out past the horse, chopping with his horns, looking for a target on which to use them. The second matador was in his path, the cape spread wide in both hands, scarlet toward the bull and bright gold at the back.

When the bull charged, the matador's feet jerked nervously and he snatched the cape quickly away from the horns. There was silence from the stands, except for a few jeers. There, Manolo thought, it had showed. His thin lips parted in a cold smile, startling in one so young.

The same thing happened with the next charge and the jeering from the stands grew louder. From his seat Manuel saw the matador as only a small figure in gold and black, but he knew that the sweat was running heavily down his face and that his hands were cold and wet. He was not sorry for him. Rather was he happy, really very happy that it was happening this way and the matador was afraid. Before he completed the series of abject passes the first cushions had fallen close to him on the sand and the jeering and insults were very bad.

A man and a woman seated in the shaded *barrera* seat looked at each other when the matador jerked away from the bull. They were in the first row, directly over *callejón*, the narrow passageway between the grandstand and the *barrera,* where the bullfighters stood when not in action.

The man turned to the woman with an ironic smile.

"The fans are getting on to the handsome Rodriguez," he said.

The man was Dionisio Veneno, former matador and now one of the leading managers of bullfighters in Spain. He was a man of medium height and squat figure, dark-skinned, heavy-featured with small brown eyes set under heavy bony brows. His clothes were expensive and conservative: a dark blue suit, a white shirt, and a striped tie. The first matador on the program was having difficulties with his manager and this was the reason for Veneno's presence at the *corrida*. Veneno never went to a bullfight unless it was for business reasons. When he was a youth he had been much moved by them, but his first horn wound had cured him of this dangerous sentimentality. His mistress' great attachment to the spectacle was a source of amusement to him.

Mercedes had been a dancer until she took up with Veneno. She was not a beautiful woman. Her face was plain, square, brown, with a rather wide short nose, wide mouth with a heavy underlip, heavy eyebrows that she did not pluck, and large shining brown eyes. Her hair was black, parted in the center and curled down over the nape of her neck.

It was her body, however, that caught the eye and, having caught it, held it. It was rich and full like a grape at harvest-time, the blood seemed to push against the smooth browned skin, stretching it taut like a full wineskin. She was wearing a simple black dress whose wide V was cut down from almost bare shoulders to the deep hollow between her breasts. Her arms were bare, browned, and round, and she wore a heavy silver bracelet on her right wrist and a silver ring with a large amethyst on the ring finger of her left hand. She was a woman of twenty-eight.

"He is very brave in the café," she said to Veneno. "The bravest of the brave with a bottle on the table."

"And with Mercedes at the next table," Veneno added.

"*Qué va!* I meant nothing when I said he was handsome. But he is not handsome now. He is ugly with fear."

7

"He is finished in Madrid. A fine bull, and he is ruining his chances. The handsome ones are always without honor."

The matador was finished and he walked away from the bull. It was not his bull to kill and he had a respite until the next one, unless the unexpected should happen. That the next one was his faded out of the consciousness of all in the arena now as the first matador went through his passes before killing the animal. Only two people in the arena were thinking of the next bull, the matador Rodriguez and Manuel Ortega.

Seated high and far from Rodriguez in the cheap sun-baked seats, Manuel was waiting for the next bull, paying no attention to the bull that was now being killed below him. The bull was dead and was being dragged over the sand by mules while the triumphant matador made a tour of the ring. Gradually the crowd of about fifty thousand people settled back to await the third bull of the afternoon.

The door of the *toril* was pulled open and a big black bull charged out of the corral. He stopped and stood still, alone in the bright sunlight, black and menacing. His horns were wide and sharp-pointed but not very long. A man detached himself from a *burladero,* a planked shield jutting out from the *barrera* that girdled the arena, and dashed out in front of the bull, trailing a cape across the sand. The bull charged swiftly, lowering his head to hook at the cloth, and the man dashed behind a *burladero.* The bull's horns rattled against the planks. A second man trailing a cape ran out from another shelter and the bull wheeled swiftly, charging. The man got back into the *burladero* half a step before the horns. Raging, the bull hooked at the planks, splintering them. The crowd jeered as the matador stalled behind the *barrera.*

Again, Manuel was whispering to himself. Again, let it happen again. God, let it happen now, let him show his fear. A brave bull, a noble bull, and let him show his fear. He watched the matador come out slowly, holding the cape in both hands, a step at a time, not hurrying to the horns, watched him stop some twenty feet from the bull, who stood with his flank to the red-planked *barrera,* watched him step back a few feet and then go forward

8

again, slowly, very slowly, then stop, closer than the twenty feet, watched him swing out the scarlet cloth, his body straight, his arms stiff, watched the bull gather itself, pull its forefeet together, saw its tail with the black and silky tassel lift up, saw it charge, swift, trembling, head lowered to hook. And he saw the matador's feet jerk away in an uncontrollable spasm and the scarlet cape flung up high to send the horns away from the body that shrank from the beautiful thing, the dangerous thing.

The shrill jeer of the crowd was far from Manuel now, a distant thing no longer important to him and shut out by what was close to him. He was exultant, lifted up by pride and belief suddenly in his destiny, his black eyes glittering. He saw the fear again, but now that it was there, unmistakably there, he was beyond it, obsessed with himself and what he had to do, caught up with the hopes and the hungers that bit and tore at him and gave him no peace. The plan, which had been vague, hardened now, fixed on a point in time, a place in space.

It was to be here on the gray-tan sand of the Madrid arena under a high cloudless sky of blue. After the picadors, he told himself. Then he will come out and ruin it again. And then it would be his time, Manuel's time. After the picadors and before the *banderillero*. When the trumpet blew, it would blow also for him. He heard no other sound now, his concentration wrapping him in loneliness, cottoning him off from the crowd around him.

It happened. The cruel jeers, the mocking insults were his signal, and he slipped rapidly down the aisle. As the man on the sand sent the bull away with a last upward fling of the cape Manuel was at the railing. He vaulted it lightly, a cape hanging over his shoulder. He landed softly on the sand of the *callejón*, gripped the top of the *barrera*, swung up and over that also, easily, intent, not seeing the policeman of the Guardia Civil start for him too late, feeling the hot sand underfoot, standing for a moment to get his bearings.

Then he was running toward the bull, pulling the cape from his shoulder, running toward the horns on which rode his destiny, hearing the surprised shout of the crowd, running toward the bull and stopping, closer than twenty feet, nearer then, stopping and planting his feet firmly, shaking out the threadbare cape whose washed-out redness scarcely gleamed in the sunlight, catching the bull's eye.

"*Toro*," he shouted crisply. "*Toro, ju, toro!*"

The bull's tail went up, his left ear twitched, and then he was upon him in a hot rushing charge, horns lowered, seeking him but finding the cloth instead. The crowd's *Olé* was humorous, a jeer at Rodriguez and nothing more. Again he did it, starting closer this time, trying to move the cape slowly, holding his ground, seeing the wet sheen of the blood pumping out of the animal's torn shoulder, seeing the wet muzzle and the coarse hairs under the neck, feeling no fear but only pride, a fine sweet heady pride that his feet had remained firm and that all had seen it.

Then the bull was away from him, lured by the flopping capes of the matador's assistants, and the red-shirted *monos* were running out to get Manuel. He did not run away but waited for them, holding the cape, head up, facing the crowd proudly, waiting for them to grab him and hustle him out of the arena. He wondered if anyone had noticed him, anyone important.

"Lousy amateur," the first *mono* said. "Goddamned lousy amateur."

He grabbed Manuel's arm and yanked the cape out of his hands.

"Belmonte," said the second *mono,* grabbing his other arm. "Another Belmonte. Always the Belmontes, jumping the *barrera* and waving a rag at the bulls."

Veneno smiled sardonically as he watched the confused scene directly below him. He pointed at Manuel.

"Rodriguez deserved it," he said to Mercedes. "He deserved this amateur showing him up."

"He has a good build, Dion," Mercedes said.

Veneno looked at her and then at Manuel, being pushed from the ring. He laughed shortly, derisively.

"Another handsome one," he said.

She looked at Veneno and then back to Manuel. Her browned face was composed, impassive.

"This is a proud one, this amateur," she said. "See how he holds himself! The arrogance!"

Veneno waved his hand at her. "Leave off about the amateur," he said.

"I have a feeling about this one, Dion," she continued. "He will be much man. He has the build and he has the arrogance and he has the hunger. Such make the great ones."

"Always the handsome ones," he ridiculed.

"Go bail for him, Dion," she said.

He stared at her and laughed. "Woman, you are sentimental. I did not expect it of you."

"You came to see Picota," she pressed, "but this one will make them forget Picota. Dion, do this for me, please."

"If he were a woman, well, then, perhaps. But I have no use for him."

She paid no attention to his jibe. "Let him be mine," she said.

He laughed, harder this time. "What would you do with a matador? It would cost a thousand pesetas and he will probably be gored in his first fight. I have plenty of apprentices. I need bullfighters, not untrained kids."

"For me, Dion."

He looked at her, his eyes shrewd, calculating whether he would gain more by yielding or by refusing.

"I'll think about it."

She said no more, knowing she had won.

The *monos* handed Manuel over to a couple of guards in the callejón. One of them grabbed his arm and twisted it up behind his back. Manuel gritted his teeth and held silent, hating them and despising them, but not willing to show them any pain. This he had expected and it had not deterred him and now it caused him no dismay. It was part of the gamble.

"The cape," he said. "It is mine and I want it."

The guard cuffed him across the face.

"A *fenómeno,*" the guard said. "I will miss the rest of the fight because of you, *fenómeno.* You can forget about capes. Where you're going you won't need any."

A girl leaned out of the grandstand and threw a flower at Manuel.

"Here, handsome," she cried. "Come and see me when you get out."

She shouted an address that was lost in a sudden roar from the crowd. The guard grinned at Manuel.

"You're lucky," he said. "You want to play with the bulls. That one of the flower, did you see the cape she had before her? She is the woman of Rodriguez, the one you shamed. If I were Rodriguez I would go bail for you and make an *estocada* in your belly. Serve your time and forget the bulls. You'll save yourself a goring. Flowers from a *puta!*"

They were under the grandstand now in the shade and it was very cool suddenly. They got mean again, twisting his arm badly and kicking him, but he would not show that he even felt it. He hated them, had always hated them, and someday he would show them. Now he despised them for the needless brutality.

By the time they got him to jail and were finished booking him and all the rest it was growing dark and cold. They threw him into a cell alone and he sat down on a bunk, cold in his shirt sleeves, wrapping himself in the worn blanket and sitting hunched up, trying to keep warm. Maybe someone noticed him, Manuel thought. Maybe now he would get his break.

Chapter Two

He had sat in the jail for two nights and one day and it was the morning of the second day, shortly before noon, when Manuel heard the guard coming down the narrow corridor between the cells. He thought he was coming with the tin plate full of hot steaming slop that passed for lunch, but his hands were empty. The guard stopped outside his cell and looked at him with distaste.

"Fix yourself, man," he said sourly. "You have a visitor." He rolled his eyes and licked his lips. "Why a woman like that should waste her time on one like you is not for me to understand."

Manuel shrugged his shoulders and remained where he was, seated in the bunk.

"I know no woman," he said. "You are mistaken. Or maybe that's what passes for fun here among you."

He spat on the floor through the bars right at the guard's feet. The guard stepped toward the cell and then stopped. He glared at Manuel but did nothing, and it was then that Manuel began to believe that there really was a visitor and that it might even be a woman. But he made no move to straighten his clothing, disdaining that. He was not given much time to reflect on this development because he heard the door at the end of the corridor open and the sharp click of a woman's heels on the concrete floor accompanying the heavier, duller sound of a man's steps.

In the dim light Manuel could not see her face clearly when she came into view. He looked up, not showing his curiosity, waiting to see what it was all about. The head guard gestured to his cell.

"Here he is," he said.

"Open it," the woman said. "I want to talk to him."

She was not of the respectables, Manuel thought, but was one of his own class. That he had never seen her before he was certain. The guard opened the door of the cell and Mercedes stepped in. The guard came in with her.

"Leave us," she ordered. "I'll call when I want you."

After a moment's hesitation the guard stepped out and

slammed the cell door shut. She's got connections, Manuel thought. Other things also, especially a body. He examined her furtively, not seeing the broad, plain face, but held by the roundness and the fullness of the rest of her. She was more than a gypsy girl to be caught tipsy at a fair and hustled off to a dark corner. She was examining him also and they remained silent for a few moments, he still seated, she standing.

"They call you Ortega," she said finally.

He nodded, still silent.

"Not Joselito?" She had named the greatest matador in history, but she was not jeering at him. Rather she wanted to goad him to speech, and he knew it.

"Not Joselito and not Belmonte," he said quietly. "Just Ortega. Manuel Ortega."

"I am called Mercedes," she said.

"I would offer you a seat, but our furniture is not of the best," he said.

"You want to go out?"

He shrugged his shoulders, still waiting.

"It is a wait of one month, perhaps two," she said. "Or maybe you have five thousand pesetas to pay for a fine."

His eyes flashed angrily and he got up.

"I know the penalty," he said, his voice rising "I knew it before I came here."

She nodded. "This I thought," she said. "But did you think how it was to be avoided?"

"Perhaps I did."

"Don't you want to know who I am?"

"Is it important?" he said. "No. It is enough that you are here. It tells something of you, though not all. The rest you will tell me yourself soon enough."

She smiled and shook her head slowly from side to side.

"Do not waste your arrogance on me, young one," she said softly. "I have already seen enough of it. Arrogance with a woman is nothing. How are you with the bulls?"

"The bulls? I eat them raw."

She got angry very quickly at his insolence and cursed at him in a low voice, running the curses together, including his mother and his father and any other blood relatives he might have had, the gutter words falling from her

14

mouth heavily. He stared at her for a moment and then smiled broadly. She stopped and smiled also.

"All right," she said. "Enough of this. I can see already that you are a rare one and you do not have to impress me any more. Now I must have some facts. Where are you from? By your speech, Ronda."

"Málaga," he said.

"You have fought bulls before?"

"A few times. Not often."

"A *novillero?*"

He shook his head. "Amateurs."

She nodded slowly. "No money, is that it?"

"The cape you saw," he said, "was an old one of my brother's. He's dead now."

"From the bulls?"

"No. The police."

"Better and better," she said. "What are you doing in Madrid?"

"You were at the arena?" he asked.

She nodded.

"That," he said. "That was what I was doing in Madrid."

"You came to Madrid for that?"

"For that and for no other reason."

"It is hard to believe. You could have done the same in Málaga."

"Málaga," he sneered. "Big bulls and small promoters. It would have been a waste."

"What experience have you?"

He thought for a moment.

"With some friends I used to go out to the ranches at night and pass the bulls with the cape by the light of a lantern."

Her eyebrows went up. "Gored?"

"Never."

"What of your family?"

He shook his head and his mouth turned bitter. "Dead," he said. "All dead."

"And girls?"

He laughed shortly. "You ask strange questions, Doña Mercedes."

15

"I am not Doña Mercedes," she said quickly. "Just Mercedes. And stick to answers or you will stay in this cell for half a year."

"No money," he said coldly. "No girls."

"That's better," she said. "Watch your mouth or I will forget about it and that will be the end of it and of your trip to Madrid."

She studied him in silence and he held himself under control, knowing that the decision was coming now. He still could not figure out how a woman could be involved, but strange as it seemed, he was beginning to believe it. Nothing she said told too much, but her whole manner indicated wide knowledge of bullfighting. But he was no prize for a woman like her.

"Veneno says I am sentimental," Mercedes said, "but I think you are a matador."

"Did you say Veneno?" He was suddenly excited.

She nodded.

"He sent you?"

"Calm yourself," she said, smiling. "No. I sent myself. Veneno called me a fool for coming. You had a close call with your mouth, but it is all right now."

She went to the cell door and called for the guard, who came quickly. When she was out in the corridor she turned back to him.

"It will be finished quickly, young one," she said, "and then we will see."

In less than half an hour a guard returned and opened the cell for him and pointed to the door. No pushes, no kicks, no spitting, no curses. She had not been playing around. He was really going out and his big gamble had paid off. He should have been exultant, but instead he was filled with cold curiosity about the woman Mercedes, interested more in her than in his coming meeting with Veneno. The biggest manager in Spain. And he was not even thinking about it.

She was sitting in the room outside and got up when he came in and her brown eyes widened at his appearance. He felt self-conscious and began to be angry that she should make him uncomfortable.

"It is the same as it was in the cell," he snapped.

"You are not yet an artist," she said easily, "so hold

16

your anger to yourself. If you are to meet Veneno you cannot look like a stable boy. Have you other clothes?"

His eyes went down to the threadbare black pants, crumpled and dusty, the worn rope-soled shoes of a peasant, the sweaty shirt. He felt his face and the stubble was stiff and scratched his palm.

"A wash and a shave," she said, "and it will be all right."

She waved her hand at him, silencing him.

"You are an expensive amateur," she said with a smile. "But let's go. Veneno will be waiting for us."

He looked at the guards.

"It's all arranged," she said. "They have experience in these matters and it is not too difficult."

"Then let us go," he said. "I have no love for this place."

The sun was bright outside, and walking beside her into the brightness was something good, a new feeling for him. She used a perfume that was not too strong and he could smell it as they walked, just enough to reach his nostrils and make him want to smell more deeply of it. The top of her head was on a level with his mouth and he looked down at her, at the point of the V made by her dress.

She looked at him. "And does it please the *diestro?*"

He ignored her mockery, letting his black eyes meet her brown ones.

"If it was meant to be hidden," he said, "then I have wronged you."

She laughed. "Wronged me! I have been stared at before and by better than you."

He shook his head. "Not by better," he said.

"Richer, then."

"Richer, yes."

She opened her purse and pulled out several peseta notes.

"Well, better or worse, buy yourself a suit quickly and meet me in half an hour." She named a café. "I will be there with Veneno."

He watched her go down the street, admiring the way she walked. Then he turned away and searched out a clothing store. He bought a cheap blue suit and used the money that was left to buy a pair of shoes also, telling

17

the clerk to wrap up his old sandals. The clerk gave him the paper and told him to wrap them himself and he had to hold his anger in check. The new shoes were stiff, and by the time he reached the café his feet were hurting and he was angry about everything, about his poverty and about her sneers at it, about the clerk and his having to control himself, about having to beg and be humble in order to get his chance. He saw her sitting with a squat dark-faced man who he guessed was Veneno.

As he entered the café a man rose from one of the tables and came toward him and grabbed him roughly by the arm, pulling him around.

"So. It is the amateur who jumped the *barrera.*"

The man was a little drunk and Manuel guessed it was the matador Rodriguez, who had been afraid two days before. He pulled his arm from the other's grip, glad for a chance to let out his anger.

"There's not enough in that bottle to give you courage," he said.

Rodriguez grunted once and swung at him. Manuel sidestepped, caught the arm by the wrist with both hands, and pulled down sharply. As Rodriguez' body bent forward, Manuel brought his knee up into the matador's stomach. Rodriguez collapsed on the floor, both hands pressed to his belly. Manuel stepped over him and continued toward Mercedes. No one in the café had moved from his seat and now a waiter came up and pulled Rodriguez to his feet.

Veneno was watching Manuel as he came up, the black eyes sizing him up, cold, but a little amused at the easy way he had disposed of Rodriguez. The manager turned to Mercedes.

"He has some experience," he said when Manuel could hear. "You must give him that. The bulls of the cafés hold no terrors for him."

He gestured to a chair and Manuel sat down. "How old are you, Ortega?"

"Twenty-one."

"When?"

"October."

Veneno made an impatient gesture. "The one past or the next?"

"The next one," Manuel admitted.

Veneno shook his head and turned to Mercedes. "See? You can't trust them about anything." He turned back to Manuel. "Experience?"

Manuel started to tell him what he had told Mercedes in jail, about going to the ranches at night.

"Stop," Veneno said angrily. "What do you take me for? Save that nonsense for Mercedes. When you are a success, if that should happen through some miracle of the good God, then you can feed that swill to the propaganda sheets for the fans to swallow. I asked what experience?"

"Amateur fights," Manuel said, his face dark red. "One fight as a *novillero*."

"What happened that time?"

"Nothing."

"What do you mean, nothing?"

"I killed the bull."

"You were bad?"

"It was my first fight. Without training."

"All right, all right. It's just a word and it doesn't mean a thing to me. But if you were bad, say so."

"I was bad."

Veneno glanced triumphantly at Mercedes, who sat stolidly, showing no reaction. He grunted and turned back to Manuel.

"Listen, get this and get it straight right now. No funny business or it's back to the jail for you. This is Mercedes' idea, not mine. I do it for her. If she wants to be sentimental, I allow her to do it once in a while. You will sign your contract with me. You know who I am?"

Manuel nodded.

"Good. Now remember this. You are not free from jail. I have not paid a fine for you. I have given bail. If it pleases me, the case will be dropped. If not, you will go back. And not for a month, either, you understand? They will throw away the key."

He stopped and looked at Manuel, his stubby fingers drumming on the table, his eyes drilling hard into Manuel's. He's showing off for the woman, Manuel thought. He's trying to make me ridiculous for the woman. He said nothing, waiting for him to resume.

"The bail money, two thousand pesetas, you owe me,"

Veneno said. "All the money we spend from now on you will owe me. You will get the sheet with all the expenses on it later. When I think you're ready, you will fight as a *novillero,* a semiprofessional. You'll get the best rates because you're under my contract. Everything you make will go to pay me back until we are even. Clear? If you're gored in your first fight, I'll send you back anyway. I don't care if you get killed in the ring. That's your business. My business is to make money."

Manuel said nothing, knowing his silence was annoying Veneno. He knew he didn't like the manager, that the cynicism was not a fake but the real thing.

"Didn't they teach you to talk in Málaga?" Veneno said.

"Agreed," Manuel said.

Mercedes laughed. "Satisfied, Dion?"

"You picked a rare one," he said. "A real rare one. Already he thinks he's an artist." He pulled out his watch and got up. "You have money?"

"Two pesetas."

Veneno pulled out his wallet and flipped a few notes to the table.

"I have an appointment. Mercedes will manage you from now on. You are her property."

He went out. When he was gone Manuel called the waiter and ordered some wine.

"So you are Veneno's woman," he said to Mercedes.

"Watch your mouth," she said. "If you think Veneno is Rodriguez, you will not last long."

The waiter came with the wine. Manuel raised his glass.

"I drink to Veneno and his taste in women," he said softly.

Mercedes' eyes glinted angrily and then she smiled.

"And I drink to Veneno's woman," she said, "and to her taste in bullfighters."

Chapter Three

Veneno called for him the following morning with his car. Mercedes was with him, sitting up front, and in the back seat was a short thickset man, his face browned and leathery, with deep wrinkles and clear light gray eyes. He seemed enfolded in quiet dignity, and when Manuel got into the seat beside him he noticed that his hair was almost completely white.

"This is the *fenómeno*, Paco," Veneno said.

"Manuel Ortega," Manuel said.

"Torres," the old man said. "Paco Torres."

Now that he heard the name, he felt the elation that had not come the day before. The trainer of great bullfighters, Paco Torres, and he, Manuel Ortega, a bootblack from Málaga, was going to have him. He kept silent as the car went out of Madrid along the road to Talavera, the dust like a haze over it. A few miles out they turned off to the right and after a short drive pulled in before a large sprawling house. Manuel guessed that it was a ranch.

The host was expecting them and led them to a miniature bull ring adjoining a corral. They all went inside and Torres gave Manuel a cape.

"Cows," he said. "See what you can do."

The others took places behind the *barrera* and Manuel waited behind a *burladero*. A ranch hand swung open a door and a cow came charging out. She was black and white and no udder was visible. Her horns were as sharp as any bull's, though she was not the size of a mature bull and the horns were not so long.

Manuel stepped out and tried to pass the cow with a veronica, concentrating on keeping his arms stiff and his feet quiet. He knew it was not very good and he was angry with himself. He turned to face the cow, his face intent, his black eyes glittering. As the cow charged, his lips pulled back from his teeth and he held the cape out from his body. The horns passed close, catching in the cape, and the cow's flank bumped him as she passed. He went down and the cow whirled and was on him, bumping with her nose as she tried to gore. Torres came out with a cape and lured her away.

21

A little unsteady, Manuel faced the cow again. This time she caught him and tossed him. He flew through the air and the wind was knocked out of him. Stunned, he lay there for a moment before ranch hands dragged him out of danger.

"Well?" Veneno asked.

Paco shrugged his shoulders.

"I have seen better and I have seen worse," he said. "He has a good build and he has good wrists. The rest he can learn. About the courage—well, it is too early to tell."

"You will take him?"

"Yes. You are paying, and, as I say, he is not the worst."

Manuel got up and came over to them. "Let me have another one," he said.

Veneno shook his head. "We've seen enough. Paco here will take you on."

He looked at Torres. The short, bandy-legged man was watching him with an aloof humor, the light eyes twinkling in the bronzed face.

"Do not be deceived, boy," he said. "I have told Veneno I will take you on. This does not mean you are good. It means only that I will make you able to defend yourself in the bull ring. The rest you must do yourself."

"It is enough," Manuel said.

"Few words and much spirit," said Torres. "Good."

"He is a rare one," Veneno said.

"And a hungry one," the old teacher added.

"Hungry for money," Veneno said. "For that, we're all hungry."

"You and your money," Mercedes said.

"I and my money. They cannot be separated. We are the best friends in all the world. I am loyal to it and it is loyal to me. You too. You are loyal to my money."

For a moment her face went ugly; then she smiled, showing the strong white teeth between the red lips. Her glance shifted from Veneno to Manuel and then back to the manager.

"I spit at your money," she said. "It is made on the blood of brave men and brave animals."

"Also on the cowardly," he chuckled. "On all."

The rancher came up, inquiring if they wanted another

cow. When they told him they were finished, he insisted they stay for lunch. He began to talk to Veneno, trying to persuade him to have his matadors demand his bulls for *corridas*. Veneno listened politely but did not commit himself.

In all this Manuel felt very much out of place. It began when they were talking about him and it grew when he saw Veneno trying to lower Mercedes in his eyes. Now at lunch with the rancher he was an extra, a boy who wanted to be a bullfighter, tolerated only because he was with the others. No one spoke to him during the meal. He excused himself before the end and went outside, wandering over to the corrals, beyond which he could see a herd of bulls roaming the hilly pasture. He thought about what had happened in the past few days, recalling the hectic moments at the bull ring, the day of despair in the jail when it had all seemed wasted, and now his success, the occurrence of the one-in-a-thousand chance.

It did not satisfy him. He could not be patient and wait for the process to complete itself, for the pattern to be revealed. He wanted it all now. Hungry, Torres had said. Yes, he was hungry. Hungry for it all; for money to make him forget the days without food and the nights without shelter, for women to make him forget the jeers of other women, for the fawning admiration of the hangers-on to make him forget the hundreds of snubs, kicks, bruises, and hardships of a resentful poverty, for the fame to recompense him for having been nobody all his young life.

Most of all he was hungry to reveal himself as the man he was, not a boy with a foolish ambition, but a man who could face death, who could deal death. He wanted to wrest from the world an acknowledgment of his manhood, to ram it down their wildly yelling throats, to revenge himself for the world's indifference to him. He would show them all! Veneno, first of all. Mercedes too. Even the rancher who would not speak to him.

They came out later without seeming to have missed him. He saw Mercedes flirting with the rancher as Veneno looked on, bored. Paco came slowly to him.

"Come on, kid," he said. "We're going back to Madrid. Tomorrow you will meet me at the Casa Florio after breakfast and we will begin. If you want to get drunk, do

23

it tonight. Tomorrow the work begins. If you drink or if you chase after women, I won't work with you. After, you can do as you like."

Manuel arrived at Casa Florio early the next morning. It was an outdoor restaurant with a sunken clay arena at the back where the bullfighters came to practice. Paco led him back to the arena. He had a wicker basket, which he set down on the ground. Out of it he took a fighting cape, which had not been cleaned and was still stained and stiff with blood.

"First," Paco began, "whatever you have learned you must forget. If I am to form you, it must be as if you were a newborn babe. Hear this and hear it well. You must forget about your legs. They are nothing to you. They serve to carry you out to the bull and to carry you around the arena after the bull is dead. Between those two moments your legs mean nothing."

He held up his arms.

"Here is your weapon. The bull has his horns and his strength. You have two wrists. In them lies everything, defense and attack. Learn to use them. The great ones are all wrists and heart. The good ones are all wrists and some heart. The dead ones are all heart and no wrists. Remember this. Now, we begin."

He led Manuel to a fence that ran around the arena, the same height as the *barrera* in a regular bull ring.

"Hold out your arms so."

He pushed his right arm out straight from the shoulder and brought his left arm stiffly across his chest with the hand below the right elbow. Manuel imitated his movements.

"Feet together," Paco snapped.

Manuel brought his feet together. Paco nodded and handed him the cape. Manuel repeated the gesture with the cape.

"Now to the other side, but slowly."

Manuel tried. Paco took the cape from him and showed him how to do it. Then Manuel began to practice the movement with the cape, from left to right and right to left, moving his body only from the waist up, practicing while the sweat ran down him and his arms and shoulders

24

ached. Paco said nothing, seating himself at a table, chatting with other *toreros* who came in, occasionally glancing over at Manuel. After almost two hours of this he came back to Manuel.

"All right, that's enough for now. Come over and sit down."

Manuel's arms trembled with fatigue, but Paco acted as if it were nothing. He also was trying to humble him, Manuel thought. He decided he would not admit that he was tired.

"That is the veronica," Paco said. "Forget all else you have heard of the veronica. That is it. You must practice it until you would do it if a bull rushed you in your dreams. From that flows all else. When you have learned that, then we will work with animals. Until then we stay here."

This went on for a week. Manuel came out in the morning, practiced with the cape for two hours, rested for an hour, and then practiced again for two hours more. After that he went to the slaughterhouse, where he killed bulls with a short dagger stroke behind the ears. He watched the bulls skinned and dressed, learning all he could about their anatomy. He came out smelling of the slaughterhouse, hating it. He saw no one except Paco, since he had no friends in Madrid. He lived with his lessons, practicing before a mirror when he went home late in the day.

After his seventh day of lessons Paco announced that they were leaving Madrid the next day.

"Kiss your girl good-bye, boy. We go to a ranch now to learn the business on live cattle."

"It's about time," Manuel said coldly.

Paco stared at him and shook his head from side to side. "Meat for the bulls," he said.

Chapter Four

The ranch of Don Eduardo Cofiño was located several hours drive from Madrid, off the main road at the end of a bumpy, dusty, climbing road that twisted through fragrant groves of pine and rough meadows covered with short grass.

Manuel had seen big manor houses like this before, but always from the outside. It was a stone house, more like a fortress than a home, and the scarred gray stone showed that it had been used as a strong point at least once during the Civil War.

Don Eduardo came out himself to greet them and to Manuel's surprise gave Paco the *abrazo,* embracing him warmly. Standing together, Don Eduardo and Paco were the two sides of Spain, the one an old aristocrat, tall, his light skin browned by the sun but still soft, his hair all white and combed neatly, his rancher's dress casual but expensive, decorated with silver; the other, Paco, was a peasant son of people who had been peasants for hundreds of years, short, bandy-legged, dark-haired, his skin also browned deeply by the sun, but made tough and grained like old leather, his movements abrupt where Don Eduardo's were smooth, his voice grating and the words slurred, where Don Eduardo gave a melody to all he said.

Yet in them both was dignity. It was a lot of dignity for such a place, Manuel thought. There was more dignity here then he had ever seen before, and he was a little irritated by these two old men encased in self-satisfaction. He would have traded all their dignity for a glass of cold wine.

"Well, Paco, it has been more than two years," Don Eduardo said. "Time has treated you easily, I see. And still hoping for another great one. Well, that is good. Good. It is hope that sustains us all in these days."

"This is the young one of whom I wrote, Don Eduardo. Manuel Ortega. He is the protégé of Veneno."

Don Eduardo's face clouded. "Veneno. Well, he is not one to waste a peseta, though I do not like his methods." He turned to Manuel. "So this is the coming Joselito," he said, not mocking, but with good humor and a little con-descension. "Paco wrote that he has high hopes for you."

"He hasn't told them to me, Don Eduardo," Manuel said.

He hated being humble and keeping his place with these aristocrats. It was bad enough with Veneno and his type, but with them it was business and could be borne. This one had nothing for him and yet he must keep his voice low and act grateful.

Don Eduardo led them inside and a fat woman bustled out with a bottle and glasses on a tray.

"You must be thirsty," Don Eduardo said. "Here. This is our own vintage."

He poured for them all and handed them the delicate stemmed glasses.

"To the brave festival!" He raised his glass in a toast.

A real bug, Manuel thought, an old fool with manners fit for a court and using the old words that tried to hide the money behind it all. He raised his glass to Don Eduardo's and drank his wine thirstily. It was cold and red as he wanted it and without any lingering sweetness after it was down in his belly. He had contempt for Don Eduardo now that he saw how he was about bullfighting. All his life he had seen them, for many more years than Manuel had been alive, and he still fooled himself about the money and the bravery. A rich old man, he thought, with nothing better to do than raise bulls with sharp horns and to run to *corridas* to watch bulls and men die. The sight of blood probably kept him alive.

At dinner that night he found out about the friendship between Paco and Don Eduardo. Paco had saved his life. Don Eduardo had been a matador and still bore the scar where the horn had caught him that day. Paco had pulled the bull from him and taken a wound himself as a result. It had meant the end of Don Eduardo as a matador be-cause his family had refused to allow his return to the ring and had used their influence to keep the promoters from booking him. He had finally reconciled himself to retire-ment from the bull ring, but he had become the patron of many aspirant matadors and his great hope was to dis-cover a genius. Many had come but all had failed to reach the top and the hope was growing dim now. Manuel

27

was given a room of his own. There was a big wide bed, four-posted and of dark mahogany. At the side of the room was a fireplace with logs piled neatly beside it for his use. The room was at the back of the house and through the narrow window he could see out to the dark rolling meadows that were bathed in moonlight. Though it was late in June it was cold here, almost cold enough for snow, and Manuel could see the vapor from his breath fogging the window. Outside someone was strumming on a guitar and singing softly.

For the first time Manuel felt he had moved out of his old life and had taken a step toward the new. The room, the fine dinner, sleeping in this big bed, and the peace of looking out over the wide meadow made him feel closer to his goal. Whatever that was, he thought. To be a killer of bulls. It was as vague as the yearnings that drove him on.

He thought of Mercedes and Veneno. Veneno he would get rid of quickly, as soon as he made his reputation and had paid him off. He felt no gratitude toward the man, only dislike and contempt. And he hated him for trying to make him ridiculous in front of Mercedes and it was not something he could forget or forgive.

And Mercedes was another thing. He knew what she was and faced it squarely, yet it did not bother him. She was the honest mistress of a crook. Manuel knew what it it was to have nothing and he did not blame Mercedes for getting what she wanted in any way that she could. He too was doing the same. He fell asleep in the wide bed thinking about her.

In the morning, when it was still cold and dew was still very wet, he went out and saw the ranch coming to life. The Cofiño ranch was completely equipped for all aspects of raising bulls, including a complete bull ring, half the size of a regulation ring. There were several rows of seats around the high wall, but only Don Eduardo was seated up there now when Manuel went out with Paco. Ranchers in their short leather jackets and wide-brimmed gray hats were their helpers.

"The fighting bull," Paco said, "is a wild animal. You saw them in the fields and when they were together they are peaceful enough. But alone a bull will attack anything without provocation. He is ignorant of man, and he must

28

remain ignorant until the moment he enters the bull ring. For a bull learns quickly and he never forgets what he has learned. If a bull knew anything of men before he entered the ring, he would charge the man and not the cape, and all the man's skill would avail him nothing.

"It is the art of the matador to control the bull's charges. The secret lies in motion. What moves will be the bull's target. What remains motionless he will ignore. If you are still and only the cape moves, controlled and directed by your wrists, then and then only will you dominate the bulls. Remember this always."

Manuel stood behind a *burladero* waiting for a cow to come out. He would not face a bull until an actual fight. A door was swung out and a roan-colored cow charged out swiftly and ran around the arena, hooking at her own shadow. Manuel waited until she had stopped and then stepped out slowly into the arena, holding the cape stiffly in both hands. He was very conscious of Don Eduardo watching him and he had the feeling that this was the day he would prove himself. He planted his feet firmly and slowly swung out the cape for the veronica to the left. The cow gathered her feet and charged explosively, horns lowered to hook. She followed the cape perfectly, the horns passing less than a foot from his belly.

Don Eduardo shouted, *"Ole."*

Manuel went through the series of veronicas, the only passes he knew, and then sent the cow away with a toss of the cape. Don Eduardo was on his feet applauding.

"I thought he was an apprentice," he shouted to Paco. "We will have a fiesta at the end of the week and Don Manuel will entertain us."

Paco's eyes were scornful and now Manuel saw the peasant show clearly in him.

"See," he said quietly, "a few passes with the cape and already you have become Don Manuel. Later you will become an emperor and then, still later, after your first bad day, you will again resume the identity of Manuel, *hijo de puta.*"

They worked daily and Paco kept him at it, driving him until the sun was too hot. They went through the cape, learning the intricate passes, the dangerous ones, a complete repertoire. And all with live cattle, experience that could not be bought. Then they passed to the muleta, the small scarlet triangular cloth fastened to the notched stick, the difficult thing and the dangerous thing with which the matador's art reached its apex, beginning with the *pase de la muerte,* the pass of death, and ending with the sword thrust. He did all but kill, holding a sword in his right hand as he went through the passes, learning to do it all, working on style and grace and skill at the same time. He knew he was making progress and with the knowledge came greater eagerness. He devoted himself to his practice with a seriousness that could not be deflected and his confidence grew.

The week passed quickly and on the morning of the fiesta he came out to see ranch hands setting up big tables on the wide grassy lawn in front of the house. He would not work that day, except to give an exhibition of what skill he had learned. The great fires were prepared and the spits set up and the platters set out, and then, finally, just before he was to give his exhibition with three selected cows, the fires were lit and the sides of beef and the whole hogs were set to turning slowly over them.

Mercedes arrived just then, in Veneno's car but without Veneno. One of Veneno's associates was with her. As she stepped out of the car she saw Manuel and her broad face grew warm with a smile. She seemed altogether in place here, bareheaded, in a blouse of much embroidery and a simple wide black skirt and sandals on her feet. In Spain, Manuel thought, none is far from a peasant.

"So you came," he said, going up to her.

"What then, my *torero?* Did you think I would miss your debut? It was I who was your discoverer and no one else."

The way her black hair curled over her neck moved him. He had worked hard all this time and the thoughts he had of her had been buried under sweat and aching muscles. His eyes went over her full body and then came up to her face. She laughed at him, far ahead of his thoughts.

"And where is Veneno?" he asked.

"Too busy," she said.

"He should look after his interests himself."

"You are not yet an interest of his."

"But of yours?"

30

"We shall see. Perhaps an interest and perhaps a boredom." Her eyes were veiled when she said it.

He grinned. "It is a long way to come for boredom. Perhaps you came to see me gored?"

Her face went very serious and she turned and rapped her fist on a wooden gatepost.

"Don't make jokes," she said, her voice husky. "I have seen it with enough matadors. It is asking for bad luck to talk in this way."

He was satisfied to have upset her aplomb and went off to the arena. There were to be three cows and he would work with cape and muleta. All the ranch hands piled into the seats girdling the arena, and when all was set Don Eduardo gave the signal for the first cow to be let in. Manuel went to work seriously, his arrogance showing at once in the way he stood and walked. He was as good as a man could be after the short time he had worked and they applauded him without stint.

Then they went out to the tables and the fiesta began with much eating and drinking and music and dancing, first the girls and then the men, the girls with their skirts whirling high and their hair flying, brown arms and white thighs, dancing and singing and running off.

"I too can perform, *fenómeno*," Mercedes muttered to Manuel. "Watch."

She stepped away from the table and into the center of the circle. At a beat from a guitar she began slowly to stamp her feet, whirling, arms overhead, her feet moving in an intricate pattern of small steps, her body twisting, first to one side and then the other, all the time her feet and her arms moving, the skirt whirling higher, the mouth open and the white teeth bright, faster and faster till all were beating the rhythm of the dance with their hands, whirl, step, stamp, and kick, in patterns repeated as the music grew faster and louder, and then sank slowly to the ground, arms covering her head.

Her eyes were bright as she came out of the circle, her face flushed. All the passion Manuel had guessed she had showed now. He felt his throat ache as he looked at her. He walked away from the fiesta out toward the meadow, kicking irritably at clods of earth. Then he heard her following and he kept on, not turning back, but slowing down so that she could catch up with him.

"You did not like the dance?"

He looked at her somberly, his thin face dark and gaunt-looking, his eyes bright black, seeing the blood beating in her neck and the dampness of her chest where the sweat was drying, smelling the scent of her, feeling the terrible closeness of her and the warmth coming from her.

"I liked the dance."

He turned and walked on with her behind him, both walking quickly, through the stubbled grass that was already turning brown, beyond the big house and going toward a clump of trees behind which the sun was already beginning to sink.

"Then what?" she asked.

They were at the trees.

"This," he said.

And then he caught her to him and his mouth was on hers, hard, hurting, his beard scratching her brown skin.

"This, and this, and this, and this," he murmured through the kiss, hands seizing her, feeling her response, but feeling more his own strength and wanting to use it.

Then the smell of her was mingled with the fresh smell of the grass and the resinous fragrance of pine needles and her flesh was hot against his flesh, shutting out light, shutting out words, shutting out past and future, leaving only the now, the now that was always and would be always.

He was still breathing hard when she smiled up at him, lazy, sleek, contented, her eyes narrow. She stretched out her arms and her body, arching it.

"You love hard, my brave one," she said.

He couldn't be angry with her now, but he did not like the sound of it. She reached out her hand and touched his face.

"So thin and so fierce-looking," she said. "Next time you will shave."

He grinned. "Not tonight," he said. "I won't shave tonight."

"Tonight it is nothing. I will be in Madrid."

"With Veneno?"

Her smile was malicious. "Of course, with Veneno. Who else?"

He got up, angry, and she laughed.

32

"Before you are too angry, better fix yourself," she said.

"*Puta,*" he said.

Her eyes narrowed and she kicked out hard at him from where she lay, catching him in the thigh. As she came up to claw him he caught her arms and forced them behind her back.

"It's money," he said. "It's all for money. Everything. And what do I owe you for today?"

She spat in his face. "It was part of the lessons," she said. "The brave festival—bulls and women."

He released her and they stood glaring at each other.

Suddenly he felt a fool. His anger was not for her, but for Veneno. If he were man enough, she would come and he would not have to humiliate himself in this way.

"All right!" He kicked at the ground. "But I do not like to share a woman. I will make plenty, more than Veneno."

Her anger disappeared as quickly as it had come.

"Surely, it will be as you say. Why not? For one so young and handsome, it will all be easy."

"No Veneno," he said.

She shrugged her shoulders and went off ahead of him, brushing her skirt. He scowled as he watched her, the good feeling already gone and the old hunger, the old restlessness returning, goading him. He would have liked to use the sword now.

The older man's face had the same composure as always when he came into the hotel room. He laid his hat on a dressing table and nodded to Manuel.

"How are the bulls?" Manuel asked.

Paco glanced up at him quickly and Manuel knew it was to see if he were afraid.

"The bulls are as always. With horns and with tails."

"Big?"

Paco grunted in reply. Manuel guessed that they were big and Paco didn't want to tell him and didn't want to lie about it either. He really felt nothing in the way of fear and he would have tried to tell Paco this, but it would have seemed empty and possibly boasting, and anyway, he would not talk of being afraid because he was too proud to admit it even as a possibility. So they said nothing and sat there in the heat waiting for the day to go by so that he could go out to the plaza.

When the waiter brought up the dish of broth and the soft-boiled egg, the coffee and the rolls, it brought the fight nearer to him. This was all he would eat until afterward, so that if the horn found him and the wound were in the intestines, the surgeon could work better.

A little before noon Veneno and Mercedes arrived. To Manuel's surprise, Don Eduardo had come with them. Mercedes was as he had known her from Madrid, casual, dressed in a loose thin dress cut as low as possible, her hair fluffed out over her dark neck, the brown eyes amused and aloof. He had seen Veneno but once in the two months, when Veneno had come to see if he were ready for a fight, and now that he saw him again it was too much. The small dark eyes were estimating him, trying to see if he were afraid. Manuel's mouth showed scorn and dislike and he nodded briefly as they came in.

"How is he?" Veneno asked Paco.

Manuel got angry that he did not talk to him.

"I'm fine," he said before Paco could answer. "Better than you ever were before a *corrida*."

Don Eduardo smiled and glanced at Veneno, while Mercedes' eyes warned him to be careful. Veneno's smile was ironic.

"Save the temperament," he said sardonically. "Save it for the fans. They eat it up and pay money to see it. To

me it is nothing. When you've killed a few bulls we'll see how much of an artist you are."

"An artist with a peseta," Manuel said.

Veneno flushed and his eyes grew hard. He stepped close to Manuel, his square face set coldly.

"You want to go back to that cell? It's all right with me. I can afford the loss."

"You can afford it, but you won't do it," Manuel said, his eyes angry. "Not you. The peseta comes first. You see, you will make money and I can say anything. Anything. Go ahead, Veneno. Prove to them all I'm wrong."

"After the *corrida*." Veneno had backed down. "We'll see how big you are with your mouth after the *corrida*."

"Knock on that," Paco said shortly. "Knock on the wood."

"We'll go see the bulls," Veneno said to Mercedes. "Come on."

She saw Manuel was angry but she went anyway. When they went out, Manuel spat at the door.

"Calm yourself," Don Eduardo said. "Pride is all right, but be careful of it also."

"I don't like him," Manuel said.

"He can do much for you."

"I don't want it from him. I don't want anything from him."

"Good luck," said Don Eduardo as he went out.

Paco shook his head and scowled at Manuel but did not say anything. He went out of the room, leaving Manuel alone. When he came back a few minutes later he examined him carefully before speaking.

"You do not go to see the bulls?"

Manuel shook his head. "I'll see them in the plaza. It is enough."

Paco nodded slowly. "It is the woman," he said, as if to himself. "And with a *puta* like that one."

"Shut up, Paco."

"A *puta*," Paco repeated. "Do I not know her for ten years? I saw her first in Pamplona, after a *corrida*, during the Fair of San Fermin. She was a dancer, but also the woman of Asturias, a picador, and Pachuco, the matador, took her away. The picador worked for Pachuco but he fought him anyway and hit him with a bottle and sent

36

Pachuco to the hospital. She followed the fairs and went from one *torero* to another, staying with them until their courage departed. Then Veneno saw her and she went with him. A *puta*, a damned lousy *puta*."

"I know it," Manuel said, his voice tight. "She's a *puta* and I'm a *torero* and that's the way it is. They are also women, sometimes better women than the others."

"You know a lot about them," Paco jeered.

"Shut up. I've heard enough."

Paco laid out the rented suit on the bed. Manuel glanced at it and his anger died down. Paco was right. If it were not for Mercedes, he would not mind Veneno. But he got wild at the thought of them together, let alone seeing them together with Mercedes acting as if he were nothing to her and he himself having to play along with that game. He did not try to think about his feelings, not being that kind of man. It was enough for him that he wanted her, no matter that she was another man's mistress or that she was much older than himself or that she wanted money and would not do anything otherwise. He wanted her as much as he wanted the rest of it.

About one o'clock a breeze sprang up and pushed some of the dampness away. It worried Paco, but after Manuel got into the rented suit, black and gold and a little tight around the shoulders, it died down again and it was hot and clear, a good day for a *corrida*. They drove to the plaza in the Ford and walked through the crowd into the *toreros'* entrance. A few people—not many, since he was unknown—wished him luck. He went into the chapel with the other *novilleros*, and knelt and said a short prayer, not because he felt like praying or cared about it but because that was the way it was done.

The two other *toreros*, both *novilleros*, semiprofessionals, were aloof and did not talk to him. Paco was quiet also. One of the *novilleros* was a youth of his own age who was beginning to get something of a reputation. The other, who was cousin by marriage of the promoter, was a local man. The relationship with the promoter was enough to get him on a few cards every year, which made him a success in the cafés, but kept him poor. The first one already traveled with his own *cuadrilla*, a *banderillero* and two picadors, while Manuel and the local man would use

the regulars assigned by the bull ring.

They lined up for the *paseo* into the arena, the three fighters in front. Paco was behind Manuel, who managed to get himself the center spot, with the others strung out behind the other *toreros,* the picadors mounted and last. With his dress cape furled over his left arm, tall, slim, head high and arrogant, mouth thin and looking cruel, eyes black and very bright and sunk deep and all of him looking gaunt, Manuel caught the crowd's eyes as the music began and they marched in. He was off to a good start and now that they were in the arena with the sand hot under his feet he felt the exaltation and knew it was that which he had felt in the morning and not fear at all.

The third and sixth bulls were his to kill, a thing that was good since it would give him time to get warmed up and used to the bulls, but might be bad if the fight dragged and it got dark for the last one. He took his position beside Paco in the *callejón,* the passageway between the stands and the red-planked *barrera,* leaning on the fence to watch the proceedings. He glanced up at Veneno and Mercedes, sitting in the front row with his dress cape spread before them. They were not watching him.

The first *novillero* was pretty good. He was a stocky youth of average height and not too much grace. But he was brave and he worked close to the bull, seeming to know his business, handling the cape well, though he was a little too proud of his bravery and took every opportunity to show the crowd that he was brave.

"He's pretty good," Manuel said.

"Cheap stuff," Paco grunted, "but he'll make a living."

After the third horse was hit it was Manuel's turn to make the *quite,* to take the bull from the fallen picador and show off his skill with the cape. He got the bull away all right, but his passes were not working. The bull was big, much bigger than the cows he had worked with, and charged faster. He was disappointed and angry that he had drawn no applause.

Veneno, jerking his head at Manuel, said to Mercedes, "There's your Belmonte."

"Wait," she said. "Let him settle down."

"Ten thousand pesetas," Veneno said, grunting, "and he can't hold his arms still."

38

Paco was talking to Manuel.

"Take it easy," he said. "Slow. Don't jerk the cloth. Remember, slow, slow. Do it slow. Stick to simple stuff and do it slow."

Both the other fighters did good jobs with their bulls and when his own bull came out and Manuel walked, stiff-legged, out to face him the noise of the crowd was far away, something he seemed to hear through plugged ears. Wide horns, he thought.

"Watch him now," Mercedes said to Veneno.

"I'm watching, woman. I didn't come here because I love to travel."

The bull's tail went up and Manuel's cape swirled, scarlet in the sunlight. Again the bull charged. Five times and Manuel walked away from him, leaving him in front of the horse. The stands were silent.

"He's got the jitters," Veneno said. "Big mouth but no *cojones*."

Mercedes was silent.

"You've got nothing to say now, woman," Veneno went on. "Look at how that mouth is spoiling a fine bull."

"He needs experience," Mercedes said.

"He'll be through before he gets experience. He jerks the cloth. He'll get a horn in him and then he'll be finished. Maybe today. He'll go to jail rather than face the bulls."

While the barbed *banderillas* were being placed in the bull, Paso went up to Veneno.

"You and your letters," Veneno said to him.

"He's not used to their speed," Paco said. "I did not expect more than this. He's used to cows and he must make an adjustment. I think he will be all right."

He went away again, feeling Manuel watching him and knowing the enmity between the two men. Manuel said nothing. He watched the bull, his enemy, wounded, blood pumping dark red out of the torn hump of muscle in his neck, at bay, breathing hard and on the defensive. He took the sword and the muleta and walked out before the president's box.

"To thee, Paco Torres, teacher and friend, I dedicate this, the first bull of my life."

Make it worthy of the words, he thought, feeling the exaltation, wanting to do it as he felt it. He stopped five feet

from the wet muzzle. The bull watched him, tired, sick of failure, wanting to be sure now that there was a target for his horn, not wanting to charge unless he thought he could catch his enemy. Manuel raised the muleta in his left hand, called, *"Toro"* sharply, and let the muleta fall. The bull charged and followed the cloth as Manuel brought it up in the *pase de la muerte,* the pass of death, to open the series of passes. He heard the crowd's *Olé,* but again he spoiled it by allowing the bull to charge too far past him and had to begin again. He could not link two passes together, though he was working close, as close as the best. He was disgusted with himself.

The bull was fixed in place, his forefeet together, and Manuel sighted along the sword, aiming at the spot in the shoulder where he had to thrust it, sighting over the left horn, his own left arm crossed with the muleta in front of him, launching himself at the bull, crossing the left hand so that the bull's eyes followed the cloth, sucking in his belly as he passed the right horn, feeling the shock of the bull as it began to charge, feeling the sword go in and his hand against the wet hot hide and feeling the blood against his hand, sliding out along the bull's flank and seeing him topple and then feeling it all, everything that had been far away suddenly come close and become part of him.

The crowd was on its feet shouting and Manuel looked up, grim, unsmiling, the nervous exaltation gone and in its place the knowledge that he had killed, killed well, killed with style and bravery, that he was stronger than the bull, that death had sat on his right arm and had gone from it to the bull. He pulled back his lips from his teeth and bowed to the crowd.

Paco's eyes were wide as he came back to the *barrera.*

"Mother of God, how you sworded! And the first time!"

"I was terrible." Manuel made an impatient gesture. "I guess I was nervous, but it's over now."

He looked up at Mercedes and she waved at him and blew a kiss. She was standing and Veneno was sitting, looking at him stonily. It made Manuel lighthearted to see it and it was the last thing he needed to see, Veneno's vexation at his success.

"And now," Mercedes said to the manager, "what is

there for you to say? Whose mouth is the big one?"

Veneno was angry. "He had luck," he said.

She made a derisive gesture with her mouth.

It happened with the fifth bull. The local boy, stimulated by the competition that had suddenly developed, tried more than he was capable of and the bull, a big roan-colored wide-horned animal, reaching just a little with the right horn, caught him in the thigh and tossed him, and as he fell caught him again and the horn went into his side. Both Manuel and the other matador were there to take the bull away, Manuel kicking the bull in the snout with his foot and shoving the cape in his face. In the melee the other *torero* tipped over the fallen fighter. When he got up he could not stand. His ankle had been twisted. This and his own bull were now Manuel's to kill.

The whole package, Manuel said to himself. Everything I've got. The crowd was alive, fearful, having seen the danger. Manuel came out slowly and from the stands he was an insolent, graceful, cruel, and dominating figure, his head high, his face implacable and dedicated. He shook out the cape slowly, his feet planted firmly. The bull shot straight. Manuel did not move and did not sway and only his arms moved slowly, an inch at a time, dragging the cape low over the ground, bringing the red horn past his belly less than six inches away, holding the charge in control so that he could turn with it and bring the bull back to repeat the maneuver, doing it four times while pivoting in an eighteen-inch circle and then, pulling the cape toward him, gathering it at the hip, turning the bull short, leaving it unable to charge, fixed in place, so that he could walk away, his back to the horns, and bow to the crowd.

He dedicated the bull to Mercedes. He saw Veneno pale and turn to her and he saw her smile at Veneno, mocking, unexplaining. That too, that too!

Everything Paco had taught him came out into his wrists now. He opened the *faena* with a *pase natural*, standing close enough at the start to have reached out and touched the muzzle with his sword, keeping close, passing the horn within inches of his belly, hearing the gasping *Olé* wrenched from the nervous crowd. Caught now by a cold hysteria, he held the bull close so that its blood came off on him when it passed him, keeping the line of his move-

41

ments pure and clean, his feet together, his body pliant and suave, holding the horns close to him, passing them ten times without changing his position, and then he turned the bull sharply, not too sharply so that it would be hurt and unfit for the fight, but only sharply enough so that for the moment it was stopped, and walked away from it, letting the *Olés* roar through him, savoring them.

Back he went again, using everything he knew, leading the bull, dominating it with a slow and savage grace that expressed everything that was in him, feeling the hatred go out of him, out through his wrists to the hand that gripped the sword. And now it was death's moment, the moment of truth, and he paused to give it its due.

He stood before the bull, seeing its baffled futile hate, arrogant toward the strength he had overcome, and when he raised the sword he did not plunge in as he had done the first time, but took the three steps to the horns, took them one at a time so that they could be seen and counted, one, two, three, went past the horn so that it caught the embroidery on his suit, pushed the sword in an inch at a time, prolonging the moment, until his hand was against the bloody hide. Then he stood over the fallen thing, staring at the hilt of the sword protruding from the shoulder, the hate out of him, his left hand on his hip. Then he raised his head high and pivoted and walked with measured steps away from the bull, hearing the frenzied cheering and knowing that it was his, rightfully his, seized by his own skill and his own courage, and knowing also that he had at last come into his own.

Chapter Six

The sunny-side proletarians came over the *barrera* in a swarm after the last bull and caught Manuel before he could duck under the stands. A couple of huskies lifted him to their shoulders, and though he squirmed and kicked and tried to get away, they would not let him and set off at a run toward the big exit gate, yelling, shouting, singing. Girls were among the crowd and they threw flowers at him, but seeing them close was not so good as seeing them from a distance. The men in the crowd tried to push through to him and those that did slapped him hysterically on the back or wherever they could reach and it was a worse pounding than he had ever got from being tossed.

Finally he let himself enjoy it. It was the first time and it was the first thing he had won for himself. They carried him over the dusty street back to where the pavement began and then on to the hotel, those on the fringes shouting out his triumph to the passersby. Some of the crowd pushed into the hotel with him still on their shoulders, up the stairs into the room, where they finally lowered him to his feet.

Paco came in and looked around helplessly while hands were pounding Manuel. Paco took out a couple of bottles of wine and passed them around, and while they were being drunk Veneno and Mercedes came in followed by the hotel manager. Between them they managed to herd the crowd out of the room and Manuel let himself sit down on the bed, weary but elated.

There was a knock at the door and Veneno said, "Come in." Don Eduardo came in and walked straight to the bed and stood over Manuel.

"Brilliant," he said. "A triumph. Never have I seen anything like it. In all my years, never. Truly, you are a señor of the plaza. I am proud to have been your host."

"Thank you, Don Eduardo. I hope to kill many of your bulls."

Veneno came toward the bed but Mercedes stayed where she was. Manuel kept his eyes on her.

"I'm tired," he said. "I will see you all later."

"I must leave now," Don Eduardo said. "Good-by until another time."

Veneno and Mercedes did not leave.

"Out," Manuel said. "All but Paco, out."

Veneno's eyes went cold but he turned to go and Manuel grinned at his back. He watched Mercedes and she turned and went out slowly, reluctantly. Paco was watching him.

"Take a warm bath," he said. He helped Manuel out of the rented suit.

"We'll buy one now," Manuel said.

"You will buy many, Manolo. But it is wise not to rush."

Manuel waved his hand. "I'm in a hurry, man. I won't wait for it to come. I'll go out and get it. I've been without too long."

Paco shrugged. "So long as the honor remains unblemished, then all will be fine. But if honor goes, all will go."

Manuel laughed. "You have too much philosophy for me, old one. It must come with age. I'll bet the women were just as pretty when you were young. As long as the bull has horns and four legs and can see the cloth, it will always be fine."

"Today you had your triumph, Manolo. Tomorrow we'll talk of the mistakes."

"Then you'll stay with me, old man. It's settled."

Paco looked up. "I did not say it," he said.

"Give me your word now."

Paco hesitated. "It is hard, this traveling with a *cuadrilla.* For me it is easier to teach, for I have money saved and did not squander it as you are planning."

"*Qué va,* hard! I will make up a special bed of feathers for you, old one. I need you. Together we will reach the top. Say it now and do not make me wait."

Paco put out his hand and Manuel caught it.

"Then it is agreed."

"It is agreed," Paco said soberly.

Before he went downstairs Manuel took the rope-soled shoes he had brought with him, the same pair that he had worn when he jumped into the ring in Madrid, and cut

them to pieces with a knife and threw the remnants into a wastebasket. He grunted, satisfied, but when he saw himself in the mirror he did not like the way he looked in the suit he had bought with Mercedes' money.

Veneno, Mercedes, and another man and woman were seated at a table in the hotel's bar. As Manuel and Paco sat down a waiter in a white apron brought two more glasses and another bottle of Fundador.

The man with Veneno looked much like him, but fatter. There was a scar on his cheek that looked like a saber wound but was really from the broken end of a beer bottle. The woman with him was young and well dressed, though rather ugly and tending to fatness, and Manuel guessed it was the man's wife, which was a strange thing.

"This is Jiménez," Veneno introduced him. "He is the promoter here."

"You had a good afternoon," Jiménez said.

"We have had nothing like it here in Zaragoza since before the war," his wife said.

Jiménez shot her a nasty look and Manuel smiled and she looked confused. It was the wrong way for her to spend her husband's money. He looked at Veneno, who smiled at Jiménez and winked at Manuel.

"Ten thousand," he said to Jiménez. "Guaranteed for two fights on successive Sundays."

Veneno was in his element, money, and he was enjoying himself. He had outmaneuvered the promoter and everyone had seen him do it and he felt good. Jiménez nodded.

"All right. Ten thousand. Next Sunday and the week after."

"And none of those elephants like you had today," Veneno added. "Give the boy bulls that he can work with and he'll give the crowd days they will never forget."

"Salamancas," Jiménez said, and Veneno nodded.

The promoter got up and his wife did also. He pushed his hand across the table to Manuel, who took it.

"More triumphs," he said. "Every Sunday a triumph."

He left and Veneno leaned back in his chair, smiling broadly. Manuel watched him and then looked at Mercedes. She had not spoken to him since before the

fight and she had a preoccupied manner that did not deceive him at all. She had dressed carefully, he noticed, in a gay print dress that showed off her magnificent body and pulled the eyes away from the broad peasant face. From her eyes he could tell she had been drinking steadily.

"Ten thousand pesetas," Veneno said to Paco. "Not bad for his second fight. What do you say, old one?"

"Jiménez will make a profit," Paco said quietly.

"After the second fight we are finished," Manuel said very quietly. "You will take your ten thousand pesetas and then we are finished, Veneno."

Veneno came forward and drummed his fingers on the table, eyes bright and mouth thin and sneering. He pulled out a cigar and lit it without taking his eyes from Manuel.

"So. You are already an artist. I form you, I finance you, I start you, I promote you, I do everything, even buy your clothes, and now you are finished with me, is that it? Is that the way of the new sensation?"

"I will light a candle for you," Manuel said. "God will have pity on you."

Veneno smiled suddenly. "Can you read, *fenómeno?*"

"Careful, Veneno," Manuel said.

"Then read your contract. Read it well, all the way through, and you will learn something of interest. You think I am an amateur, that I do not know your kind? Five years, punk. Read it and learn the facts. Five years."

"Five years!"

"Yes." Veneno leaned toward him. "You must pay the percentage for five years. On every fight. If I manage you or not, you must pay for five years. You think you can play with Veneno? Try again, little boy."

"And you would do it, even after this."

"It is business. Money. Suit yourself."

Manuel knew it was true. He was chagrined at having been made foolish, at having played his hand without holding big cards. He glanced at Mercedes and then at Paco, but saw nothing there.

"Then manage," he said coldly to Veneno. "Earn your percentage. But if you try any tricks, watch out for my sword."

"Big mouth," Veneno said. He turned to Mercedes.

"Well, how do you like your *fenómeno* now? The great killer!"

"You and your money," Mercedes said.

Veneno went pale and stared at Mercedes and then at Manuel.

"You and your money," Mercedes repeated. "I spit at your money and I spit at you."

"So," Veneno said heavily. "So that is how it is?"

Manuel leaned forward. "Yes, That is how it is. You have something to say?"

Mercedes had turned the tables for him and the humiliation was now Veneno's. Out of the corner of his eye he saw Paco push his chair back prudently.

"Sleep with your money," Mercedes said. "This is the way it is and this is the way it was. Before today. Today you learn it, but it was before today. Sleep with your money."

"Puta," he said.

Manuel hit him in the face and before Paco could stop him he kicked him in the belly when he fell down with the chair clattering. Paco pushed him away and a waiter came up and stood between them. Veneno got up slowly, holding his belly where Manuel had kicked him, his face green and showing pain.

"I'll kill him," Manuel said. "I'll kill him now."

They held him and would not let him free. Veneno took a quick step toward Mercedes, but then thought better of it. She stood quietly, her eyes open wide and bright. He spat on the floor and the spittle was bloody and then he glared at Manuel.

"You will pay nevertheless," he said. "You will pay until the horn finds you. In the end there will be the horn and I will remain."

"Coward, thief!" Manuel said, raging to get at him.

"And you will pay too," Veneno said to Mercedes. "It is not something I did not anticipate and have no fear that I will pine away for you. I will buy another as I bought you."

"Kiss your money," she hissed.

"He will do it to you in your turn," Veneno said to her. "Such a one is a wolf among sheep. He will take and take until the horns take it all back."

47

He went out still holding his belly and then they let Manuel go and he sat down again. Paco remained standing.

"This changes nothing between us, old one?"

Paco shook his head slowly. "No. Your need is greater now," he said.

He went out, leaving Manuel with Mercedes.

Her eyes were still wide and her breath was coming a little fast and his eyes were on the softness of her throat and the flesh below it where it was soft and browned.

"Come," he said. "I have no desire now for wine."

"Nor I," she said.

They got up and went out together, his arm around her wasit. They went up to his room and went in without speaking.

II.

THE GLORY

Chapter Seven

Manuel gave the two bloody ears to his *banderillero*, Luis, and hustled out to the infirmary while the ovation was still loud. The door was shut and they would not let him in. One of Tono Gómez' *peones* was there, leaning on the wall, scowling.

"How is he?"

The man's black eyes gleamed hotly and he turned away and spat on the floor.

"Ask God, big shot. Don't ask me."

Manuel paled, straightened up, and turning, saw Paco shuffling along toward him. Paco stopped and asked the man who had rebuffed Manuel how the gored matador was.

"Bad," said the man. "Very bad. The horn hit the backbone."

Paco crossed himself.

"Anything I can do, call on me," he said.

The rest of the *cuadrilla* came up now and surrounded Manuel and they all went out together, surrounded by a flying wedge of guards that broke through the milling fans that blocked the exit. Men and women were sitting on the big station wagon, on the bumpers, on the fenders, and one boy even on the roof.

"Our Manolo," one shouted, "the killer without pity."

They all got into the car, and when the guards had cleared a little path the station wagon got under way at about two miles an hour, crawling and honking.

"Two ears on the last bull," Luis said. "Three altogether. What a day!"

"And Gómez in the infirmary," said another solemnly.

Paco knocked on the wood paneling outside the window and stared straight ahead of him. Manuel felt uncomforta-

able about his silence. A little angry, too, because it was spoiling his triumph in Madrid.

"I have a girl that collects ears," said one of the *cuadrilla*. "Give them to me, Luis. I'll make a big hit with her."

"A girl, he calls her!"

They all laughed.

"Be careful she does not cut your ears, Chepe," Luis said. "She is a collector, that one, but not of ears, as I heard it. You'd better stuff those ears in your pocket and leave your money home."

"Don't get caught," said one of the picadors. "Those bulls have the splintered horns."

"You married ones are jealous," said Chepe. "It's the same dish every night for you."

"As long as it's served up hot," said Luis.

They pulled up before the stone house that Manuel rented in Madrid and they all went in, still in the elaborate costumes, but not wearing their hats. Manuel went straight to his bedroom, followed by Luis and Paco. Luis started to help him out of the suit, but seeing the way Paco was, Manuel stopped him.

"Leave us, Luis," he said, "I'll call you."

Three years had changed Manuel. In appearance he was much the same, but the youthfulness had gone out of the face. He was still tall, slim, narrow-hipped, long of face, and with deep-set eyes. But there were lines in the face now that had not been there before, grooves, not yet deep, that were accentuated now by the blueblack beard that was heavier than it had been three years before. The costume made his normal arrogance even greater, the heavy gold, gaudy and elaborate, contrasting with the grim set of his face, which never smiled in the bull ring. The boy had disappeared forever.

Manolo the Killer! Sometimes the fans left off the Manolo.

"Well, Paco, what is it? I see by your face that you have a misery."

The light eyes studied him for a moment before replying. As always in a serious moment, Manuel was struck by the old man's dignity, an expression of his in-

wardness. No matter what was happening, if he were drunk or compromised by a bull, this dignity revealed itself. It protected his soul.

"Three years," Paco said slowly, "and it is as you said. We have gone to the top. There is none in Spain that can share the peak with you. You did not deceive me. Yet I would be finished with it."

This Manuel did not expect. "Why, Paco? I do not understand."

Paco waved his hand vaguely. "Don't ask an old man for reasons."

"Gómez?"

"Then you know."

"You blame me? You think I was too slow with the cape? That I did not want to save him from the bull?"

Paco did not answer. He stood, stolid, his eyes fixed on Manuel, boring into him, his face set. An old man, short, bandy-legged, looking a little silly in the fancy suit, but a man, all man, someone Manuel could not lightly dismiss.

"Well, speak, man." Manuel said it hotly, stepping toward Paco, eyes blazing. "As God knows, I was as quick with the cape as I could be."

"Do not speak for God."

Manuel turned away and paced to a window, staring out of it. When he turned back his mouth was bitter.

"You're like the crowd," he said. "You're turning on me too. They're not satisfied unless they see blood. You saw how they screamed today when Gómez got it. Only you want my blood! Three gorings in three years are not enough! But you will never see it happen to me. Not to Manolo! To hell with them all!"

"I did not say you were slow with the cape," Paco said calmly. "You were quick. And good, too."

"Then what? Because I'm up, you want to see me down? You want to build another *torero* to compete with Manolo?"

Paco shook his head from side to side. "This is what I thought it was," he said. "Where will I find another with the same combination of wrists and no pity? No, I have not this illusion that there will be another such as you in my lifetime."

51

Manuel's mouth had turned vicious. "Maybe you want more money, like the critics this year? My blood and they want money!"

"It is not your blood, but the blood of Tono Gómez," Paco said very quietly. "It is that which I cannot drink. It leaves a bitterness that can reach my soul."

"Gómez!" Manuel picked up a hairbrush and threw it hard across the room. It scarred the wall and fell quietly on the thick rug. "Clumsy fool!" he continued. "Trying things he never learned. Trying to show me up. And in Madrid, too. That's what he deserves for being stupid."

Paco put on his hat. "Good-by, Manolo. You have no need of me any longer. Luis will be a fine sword-handler."

"To hell with you," Manuel said. "To hell with you and all the others that live like leeches off the blood of matadors in Spain. I'm supposed to protect them all in the arena, to protect the lousy picador, who's afraid to shoot the stick, to protect the *peones,* and to protect Gómez, too. To protect all the other punks who call themselves *toreros* and who know only to puff out their rumps at the crowd, to wave a rag at a bull and a fancy bribe at a critic.

"And now I'm supposed to protect your goddamn soul that's got pity for everyone, that's got pity for Gómez, who wanted to show me up, for Veneno, who's still bleeding me, for everybody but me. They named me Killer, and killer I am. It's my duty to kill, and to kill well. If I killed badly, with pity, I would still be killing, only then they would call me Butcher and throw cushions at me instead of roses. I protect myself, Manolo, and all the others will have to protect themselves when they compete with me. Take yourself out of here! I'm sick of looking at that sad face. Take your face and your soul away from me because you make me sick."

Paco went out without looking back at him, closing the door quietly. The sudden quiet calmed Manuel. He stared at the door and then went to the bed and sat on it. The suit was tight and confining and the sweat that had dried on him made him uncomfortable.

Paco turning on him! That was one he hadn't expected. They all turned sooner or later. Until you were dead and then you were the best again. He'd have to make it look good with the public or they might draw conclusions.

Well, he didn't need Paco any more. He'd taken all that Paco had to give and added some of his own. An expensive hobby Paco was. Sentimentality.

He went to the door. "Luis!"

Luis came quickly. He was a medium-sized man with quick movements, a good *banderillero*. A smart lad, with small even features, he always wore a cap instead of a hat, tight trousers, and brightly colored shirts without a tie. He was married, still in love with his wife, but went to the café every night for a couple of hours before going home. He said it kept his wife guessing and made her love him more ardently.

Now his small face was glum and Manuel guessed that Paco had said his good-bys.

"You've got a long face, man," Manuel said. "You're sorry to see Paco go?"

"He knows bulls," Luis said cautiously.

"Well, it's time he went out to pasture. He say good-by to the others?"

Luis nodded.

"That's all?"

"What else?"

Well, he'd never find out what he said, Manuel knew. He gave up trying.

"Don't be sorry. You're taking his place."

Luis grinned. "Thanks, Manolo. My wife will be glad to hear it."

"Your wife! What about you?"

"But naturally. Of course, I'm glad."

"You get a raise. Take care of it yourself."

"I buy the wine tonight," Luis said. "I'm taking the boys. Is it all right?"

"Take a holiday. Two days. No more fights for two weeks. We all need a rest."

"I'll tell them."

He was tired of Luis now and wanted to be alone. Luis finished with his clothes and he went into the warm bath.

"Don't wait," he called to Luis. "I'll manage myself."

He heard Luis go out and sank back into the tub. The water and the hair on his thigh combined to make the scars there look less than they were. He touched them with his fingers, feeling the smooth hairlessness of them,

53

not remembering the pain at all. Just the thigh, the right thigh. Each time it had been the wind as he went in to kill, blowing the muleta up and toward him. Otherwise they could not touch him.

Three years. He mused over the time that had fled from him, remembering it without sadness or joy. It was time gone by, nothing more, a chronicle of events to which he had been a party. One year as a *novillero,* traveling from town to town with Paco and Mercedes, appearing in small rings, winning triumphs, ears, tails, and sometimes a hoof.

Mercedes had been a surprise. She had followed the trail without complaint, taking the dust, the weariness, the second-and third-rate hotels in stride. To her a hotel was a bed and a bed was a place where she could be with him. Without Veneno to push him actively the climb had been harder than it should have been. Veneno made dates for him, all right, but always in the provinces, always hoping for the bull that would destroy him. Paco had taken care of that end, finally. Paco and Don Eduardo, who had followed him through that first year.

When the critics came to see him finally he had been a finished matador, a complete artist with cape, muleta, and sword. Then had come fame. Overnight. It had come as he had always expected it to come, with crowds cheering him, with women flocking around, with money, great sums of it pouring in, with the fawning admiration of the dilettante rich. With the name Killer.

It was in Madrid that he had become a full *matador de toros* in the same bull ring where he had jumped the *barrera* so desperately. It was a crowning touch that gave him pleasure every time he thought of it. He heard the door to the room outside open and he knew it was Mercedes. Expecting her to come right into the bathroom, he said nothing. She did not come.

"Mercedes, is it you?"

"Yes, it is I."

He got out of the tub and wrapped a big many-colored towel around himself and came out, wetting the carpet as he walked. She was sitting on the bed, and seeing her on the rose-colored satin covering he was reminded of Zaragoza and the plain iron bed of the cheap hotel there with the pitcher of cold beer on the table beside it and how she

had laughed at his embarrassment when they had to send out to have it filled again. It had been good then, very good, and it was not the same now as it had been then and he felt a little sorry that it wasn't.

She looked fine to him at this moment. She was leaning back with her legs crossed, one swinging slightly, and his eyes stayed on the plump turn of her calf. Her browned skin was warm against the color of the bedspread, and though it had been a long time since he had ever felt desire immediately after a *corrida,* he felt it now and it made him feel better about Paco's leaving him and about what had happened to Tono Gómez. She was all that was left of what had been there in the beginning. Though Veneno still managed him and collected the 10 per cent, he never spoke to him and Paco had handled all that.

He came across the room to her and put his hand on her neck, rubbing it lightly in a way that he knew pleased her. When he bent to kiss her and the towel fell open she turned away.

"You're wet," she said.

"You will dry me," he said.

She pulled away. "After a *corrida?* It is not like you. Somehow I do not have the taste for it."

"Milk," he said angrily. "I spit in the milk of your taste."

Her brown eyes were calm and she was one person he could never intimidate with anger.

"My taste is as yours was always," she said quietly. "It is strange that today you have changed."

He felt ridiculous now because he was wearing only a towel and he went out and put on a robe before he came back. She was still sitting in the same position and he got angry again because he still wanted her.

"I am invited to an affair with the aristocracy," he said. "For tonight I shall be Don Manuel, the first bootblack of Málaga."

"It is well that you remember it," she said.

"I won't have you around to remind me of it." His eyes were cold and nasty and his mouth was formed in the same wolfish grin he wore when he went in to kill. "I go alone."

"I will bear up under it."

"What's the matter with everybody?" he exploded.

"You have not heard about Gómez?"

"What about Gómez? Is Gómez paying this goddamned *cuadrilla*, that everyone thinks of him before me?"

"Gómez is finished," she said.

He shrugged his shoulders. "Of course. He was finished when he first thought of a competition with Manolo."

"You and your vanity," Mercedes said. "That is not what I meant. He will be crippled. The horn shattered the spine and he will never walk again."

"The bulls give and the bulls take away," he said.

She knocked on wood against the footboard of the bed. Then, perhaps fearing it was not enough, she crossed herself.

"From all," she said. "They give to all and they take away from all."

He looked at her sharply. "So it is Gómez and not your tastes?" he said.

"I am afraid of it, Manolo. It is a horrible thing to play with a man's life. It is an offense to God."

He laughed. "God comes easily to your mouth. All the rest of it, is that fine with God? Has He told you all things?"

She crossed herself again and he saw that she was really upset by what had happened.

"First Paco and then you," he said bitterly. "I am supposed to protect them all in the bull ring. They all want to destroy me and you have tears for them."

"Where is Paco?"

"Gone. Gone to pasture."

"Then it is true what they are saying in the cafés."

"What are they saying?" he demanded.

"That you destroyed Gómez."

"And you believe them."

"They say you will not tolerate a rival," she continued. "They are all saying it, not only your enemies. They say you trick the new sensations into competitions, that you humiliate them publicly and force them to try the impossible. Veneno spread the story that this was the way you began, that two *novilleros* were gored the day of your first fight."

He cursed. "And you, what do you say?"

56

Chapter Five

It was Zaragoza in August, hot, damp, windless, and sometime around five o'clock Manuel was to kill his first bull. They had arrived the day before, Paco and he, spent the night at a cheap hotel, and Paco had gone out in the morning to draw lots for the bulls. This was the way it began, Manuel was thinking, without a *cuadrilla* of his own, without a peseta of his own, with a rented costume, borrowed capes and muletas, borrowed swords. And with all that it was better than most. He had been formed by Paco Torres, and even if he was green and it was his first fight, he knew more than most of them after twenty fights.

The hotel room was hot and it had not cooled off during the night and he had slept only a little and now he was sweating, itchy and uncomfortable. He peered out through the open blinds but it was too early for the streets to be crowded. Paco said that Veneno was coming up from Madrid and Manuel guessed that Mercedes would be coming also.

He knew about being nervous. It was something that was supposed to happen to them all. But he wasn't nervous. He was a little tired from the trip and from not sleeping and he was irritable from being hot. He was tense, but not with nervousness. He could not identify the way he felt and he thought it somewhat ridiculous to have any feeling about it since the *corrida* was more than eight hours off. Paco would have been annoyed to know he was not sleeping.

Paco was all right. Two months he had known him and Paco had been with him every day, working with him, bossing him, yet there had not been a bad moment between them. Manuel had thought about it and he knew he wanted Paco to stay with him after he made a success. It would cost a lot because Paco was in demand, but it would be worth it. Paco would not mind his getting rid of Veneno and he would mind his own business about every-
~~g. Except the bulls. Manuel knew he needed Paco's
~~dge of bulls.

34

She sat silent and he cursed again, continuing, pouring out words at her while she sat stolidly.

He said, "More dirt comes from the mouths of the cafés in an hour than can be cleaned away in a year. Blood and dirt are what they live on. My blood. They are disappointed that it was Gómez and not me. If it had been me, they would be drinking toasts even now to the great Manolo. If the horn catches in my suit and gives me a *paletazo* in my chest, then they will sit in safety and shout *Olé*. But if it should miss by an inch they will sit silent and later in the cafés they will say, 'See, he's become rich and he's become cowardly.' "

"But another *torero*, Manolo," she protested unhappily. "It is tempting fate."

"I suppose you're going to turn on me also. I'm the best and they all want to show me up. They are waiting for me to show fear or to get a horn in my chest. The *toreros* also. To hell with them all, the public, the *toreros*, and the mouths of the cafés. It is my blood and I will defend it in my way."

She got up from the bed and went to him, putting her hands on his arms.

"I am stupid," she said, "but this of Gómez frightens me. If you play with his life, when will it be your turn? Do not do it again, Manolo."

He pushed her away angrily. "You and your knocking on wood and your crossing yourself! I did nothing to Gómez. He was a fool who could not defend himself. He tried to work closer to the bull than I and he was caught because it is impossible. That's what he gets for trying to suck after the mouths of the cafés. To hell with Gómez!"

She shrank away from him, really horrified, crossing herself again and knocking the top of the dressing table several times. Then she came to herself, seeming to shake the mood off herself physically.

"It's enough," she said. "You will hear no more of it from me, Manolo. Do as you please."

"I've already heard too much," he said.

She went to him and put her arms around his neck.

"I did not mean it for your harm," she murmured. "I suffer when I see you in the ring."

He broke her grip and pushed her away. "I do not have

the taste for it," he said roughly. "You suffer and I enjoy myself."

Her face went sullen and he was pleased to see it because she had spoiled the day for him finally and he had taken his revenge. It was a long way from the hotel room in Zaragoza, he thought, and no one could live a thing again.

"You're crazy with your arrogance," she said. "It will yet destroy you."

"Never. Not Manolo." He laughed, feeling better now. "Calm yourself. I will have pity on them in the future, if they keep their mouths shut."

She smiled softly and went to the bed and sat on it. He shook his head.

"I told you I am invited out with the aristocracy tonight. Do not be disappointed."

"Have a care for that yourself."

Chapter Eight

The Marqués de Villaverde lived in a sprawling stone house on the outskirts of Madrid in the foothills of the Guadarramas. The house had had the good fortune of being in territory seized quickly in the beginning of the Civil War and had not been an object of battle, so it remained undamaged. Manuel drove there for a dinner party with a group of the Marqués' friends.

Manuel was a new enthusiasm of the Marqués, who had taken to following him about the country from one *corrida* to another. He was the son of an old noble family and his father had been killed in the war, which had convinced the son that no cause was worth living for unless it were pleasurable. In pursuit of pleasure he ranged the countries of western Europe with amiable perseverance. It was said of him in the cafés and the fashionable resorts that there were several gypsy tarts whom he could recognize more readily than his delicate-featured timid wife.

The Marqués came out to greet Manuel, shaking his hand warmly. He was a few years older than Manuel, shorter, dark-haired, with a face that tended toward puffiness. He had the easy manner of one long accustomed to deferential treatment.

"You were immense today," the Marqués said. "Too bad about Gómez."

"Yes, he had bad luck."

He led Manuel to a large room where about a dozen men and women were standing in two groups drinking cocktails. They were all in evening clothes, as was Manuel. Mercedes had seen him go out and the look in her eyes had not bothered him then, but now he felt self-conscious about his dress, which seemed more like a costume to him than his fighting suit. He remembered the day three years ago when Mercedes had come to the jail and how the clerk had refused to wrap his old rope-soled sandals.

He was Manolo, and because his strength and skill reflected glory on his host, he was accepted among them. But he was not of these people and he did not like himself that he wanted their acceptance, though it was something he would not yield. This also was a thing he had wanted and it was also a thing that was not as good close up as from a distance. It seemed that the world was full of things that looked good from afar.

There were but two Spaniards in the group. All the rest were foreigners, the men tall and spare, the women fair-skinned and light-haired. The Marqués introduced him as Manolo.

"Manuel Ortega," Manuel corrected him. He was pleased when the Marqués widened his eyes in surprise.

The two groups came together, gathering around Manuel. They were all holding thin-stemmed cocktail glasses. The two Spaniards Manuel recognized as friends of the Marqués, second sons of nobility, big drinkers and big chasers. He refused the cocktail the Marqués offered him, angry at being used as a showpiece for foreigners.

"Some Fundador," he said.

He shook hands with the men and bowed slightly to the women as the Marqués introduced him around the circle.

"Are they English?" he asked the Marqués.

"Americans."

Several of the foreigners smiled.

"I caught your fight this afternoon." The words came from a tall young man with stiff short sandy hair whose Spanish was correct, but lame. "It was only my second time and I couldn't really tell if you were good."

A journalist, Manuel thought. He scowled at the young man.

"You will have to ask the critics," he said. "They know all. If they decide it, I am good or bad. It was not a good fight for Gómez, that much I can tell you."

"That must be the fellow who was gored," the young man said in English to a white-haired, florid-faced gentleman standing beside him.

"Why do bullfighters wear those fancy suits, Mr. Ortega?" a plump middle-aged woman asked in stumbling dictionary Spanish.

Manuel stared insolently at her heavily embroidered gown, which was cut to reveal big masses of muddy-tinted flesh. She wore large pendant earrings of diamonds and sapphires and rings on fingers of both her hands. Slowly

Manuel let his eyes move from one adornment to the next while his grin grew wider.

"To hide our scars," he said finally.

"I thought you were wonderful."

Manuel looked around to see who had said it, because the Spanish was perfect, but there was no regional accent. She was a yellow-haired girl with large wide blue eyes, a small straight nose, a small well-curved mouth that was lightly rouged, and smooth bare shoulders. Her hair was piled on top of her head with some elaborateness.

"That is a relief to me, señorita."

Her eyes widened at the remark and her mouth parted, showing white even teeth. This was something that looked good close up. She was young, younger than he, and her skin was fair, untouched by the sun. He liked the way she looked and the way she carried herself. She took his slighting remark without reacting further. She had much pride, Manuel thought.

"What happened to the other matador?" she asked.

The others in the group around them drifted away.

"Bad, very bad," Manuel said.

"He bled very much," she said. She did not seem too affected by the thought. "Was he married?"

When she asked it he saw the plain gold wedding band on her finger.

"His wife did not bleed," he said.

"Wives sometimes bleed."

"Not from their husbands' wounds."

"Were you ever gored?" the stiff-haired young man interposed.

The girl's eyes showed annoyance. "You don't ask that," she said tartly in English.

Manuel held up three fingers. "But never badly," he said.

"They're proud of it, Anna," the young man said to the girl, also in English.

"The blood gave you a thrill," she said, still in English. Then in Spanish: "The conversation has become too bloody."

She was his wife, Manuel decided, but he did not know how to handle her. Spoiled and rich. His eyes on Anna, he said. "Did you like the *corrida?*"

"Very much," she said. "Except the goring. I did not like that."

"I find it brutal," the young man said.

Manuel began to dislike him very much.

"You would," Anna said in English. "Charles Humboldt finds the bullfight too brutal. It isn't neat enough to fit into a dispatch case."

Manuel watched the exchange with interest. He did not know the words, but he could read scorn on her face.

"Cut it out, Anna." Charles Humboldt's lean face, which now seemed surprisingly weak and feminine, was flushed, and his pale gray eyes darted quickly around to the others, who did not show they had heard his wife's sneer.

"To the bull it is all the same," said Manuel, "a slaughterhouse or a sword. In the arena he has a chance to get revenge."

Dinner was in a long room decorated on one wall with a large tapestry showing knights in combat; other walls bore a series of frescoes portraying scenes of rustic life several centuries ago. One of them showed a matador citing a bull with a cape. The table was a long one and the Marqués sat at the head of it with Manuel at his right. The dishes were inlaid with gold and all the serving vessels were of gold with intricate carving on the metal. Anna and Charles Humboldt were across the table from Manuel, Anna at the Marqués' left, while the plump woman who had asked him about the fighting suits was beside Manuel.

He did not get a chance to talk to Anna during the meal. In the few brief moments he snatched while the plump woman caught her breath, Anna was being occupied completely by the Marqués, who was paying a lot of attention to her. Manuel got angrier as the minutes passed, trying very hard to insult the plump woman, but failing because she could not understand the insults. He knew that the seating was no accident and he decided to revenge himself on the Marqués. The latter was saying something to Anna, when Humboldt told her something in English, but when she replied his face got a very tight look.

Manuel felt contempt for Humboldt's weakness with a woman. But Anna deserved better than the Marqués, he thought. And he himself, he deserved something after his tough day. Paco, Mercedes, and now this fat talking machine on his right. Had it not been for the yellow-haired American girl, he would have walked out on the Marqués and his dinner party.

She had drunk a lot of wine during the meal and her cheeks were flushed and her eyes were bright when they trooped out to another room, where an automatic phonograph was playing dance music softly. He could tell she wanted to dance but he did not care to please her. Humboldt was watching her tensely.

"What do you like best in the *corrida?*" he asked her.

"The capes."

"I like the killing," he said.

"Why? The bulls seem so noble."

"The bull is my enemy. When I kill him I feel good. But you are right. The bulls are the only good ones in the arena."

"No," she said. "You're good. You're very good. I come alive when I see you go in with the sword. My chest feels very tight every time I see it."

He looked at her fine bosom when she said it and she bore his gaze without self-consciousness and then he looked at Humboldt, who had gone quite pale.

"And how does your husband feel about it?"

"He thinks it's brutal." She laughed. "I made him come, but he was disgusted."

"You're talking nonsense," Humboldt said in English. "And I know why you're doing it."

"I do not like it when you talk English." He faced Humboldt, arrogant and disdainful.

"Shut up, Charles," Anna said. "Croquet is your game." She turned to the Marqués. "I think it would be nice to go to a café now. Or am I being rude?"

"Not at all, not at all. I think it's a good idea."

"I could do without it," said Humboldt.

"It's a fine idea," Manuel said.

"See, it's all settled, Charles," Anna said.

"You'll come in my car," Manuel said to Anna. As an afterthought he added to Humboldt, "You also."

She sat between the two men while Manuel drove. He looked at her and then out at the road, dark except for the swath of his headlights. It would be all over Madrid in the

63

morning that he was running around with rich tourists.
Villaverde and Paco. Put that way, he'd made a bad exchange. He was done with that, however, and he did not
care what the mouths of the cafés said. He was Manolo,
no longer a bootblack from Málaga, and he was not one
of the boys with Paco or any other *torero*. He could
dominate life as he dominated a bull, living it as
dangerously and brilliantly as he chose. The car pulled to
a stop before an awning and a doorman pulled the door
open for them.

"This isn't a café," said Anna, "it's a night club."

"The wine is better here," Manuel said.

"That's what Charles would say."

"That's what I say," he said coldly.

"This isn't what I wanted."

Manuel got out of the car and walked away without
waiting for her. She watched him go and Humboldt began
to smile. That settled it for her and she scrambled out after him, Humboldt following along. Manuel was already
being conducted to a table as she came in and she saw
people stop talking as he went by and turn to watch him
as he moved toward his table.

Manuel saw her coming and smiled. The husband was
still there also. What kind of man was that? he asked himself. The woman thought she could use him as bait against
her husband and the Marqués thought he could use him as
bait for the blonde, but they were all following the bait
and he himself was the trapper. The band swung into a
tune written in his honor and then the manager came up,
elbowing the headwaiter aside, and showed them to a
table.

"This place is like a copy of Broadway," Anna said.

"Broadway? What is that?"

"New York."

"Good," he said. "Now I do not have to go to New
York."

The band started up an American dance tune.

"That's for you," he told her.

"I want to dance," she said.

Manuel looked at Humboldt and started to get up.

"He can dance with the Marqués," she said.

Manuel froze where he was, thinking. Now it's going to

64

happen, now he will show he has had enough. A woman never knew when to keep quiet. He saw Humboldt turn pale and his fists clench, but the man did nothing. It would never happen, Manuel decided. Not with this one.

"Careful," the Marqués said to Manuel.

Manuel grinned at him. *"You* be careful," he said.

Anna laughed. Humboldt did nothing, continuing to stare miserably into space. Manuel held out his arms and the girl came into them, holding her face up to his, her eyes glittering. He started dancing with her at the table and moved her out between the other tables toward the dance floor. Over her shoulder he saw Humboldt slumped in his chair while the Marqués was catching the eye of a girl at the next table.

"You're a good dancer," Anna said.

"No. I'm a rotten dancer."

"All right. You're a rotten dancer."

"You want to stop?"

"Now you're being nasty to me," she said. "Please don't."

Charles was watching them when they came back to the table. To Manuel he looked terribly beaten.

"Isn't he handsome, Charles?" Anna said in Spanish. "Isn't he terribly handsome?"

The Marqués was at the next table with the girl he was trying to attach and the three of them were alone. Manuel waited for it now, feeling strong and confident, not caring about consequences.

"I thought we weren't going to have any more of this," Charles said in English. "I thought you were going to stop acting like this."

Manuel stood up and leaned over the table toward Humboldt. "Talk Spanish," he grated, "or shut up."

"See, Charles," Anna said in Spanish, "that's how a man acts. But you wouldn't know about that. I am not a good woman, Charles. Being with you makes me worse. I surely am a bitch, but what can I call you?"

"You said it would be different," he said, flushing, still in English, ignoring Manuel. "You said you wouldn't."

Manuel slapped his hand down hard on the table, sick of this whining shadow of a man who didn't know how to control his woman.

"See," Anna said, "I can't help it. Isn't that what you told me about yourself? You were a big disappointment to me, Charles."

Humboldt got up. "I'm leaving," he said.

"I'll see you later," she said pleasantly.

He stared at her for a moment and Manuel was sure he saw tears in his eyes.

"You'll pay for this," Humboldt said, and he walked out stiffly.

Anna picked up her glass and held it out for Manuel to fill. She did not seem as sure of herself now as she had before. He reached out and took the glass from her hand and set it down.

"No more wine," he said. "Let's go."

Chapter Nine

It was an inn in Talavera that had a reputation for this kind of rendezvous and the proprietor started hopping around when he saw Manuel with Anna, bustling and rubbing his hands together while his sly eyes roamed over Anna. It had to be here because Mercedes was in the house and any place in Madrid would have made it public knowledge within the hour.

"Don Manuel," the proprietor gushed, "Don—"

"Enough of this Don Manuel," Manuel told him. "I want quiet and I want silence. Discretion, understand? If I hear a word about this in Madrid I'll come back personally to slit your belly. Now give me a good room and get a bottle of manzanilla and make it quick. Clear?"

"At your orders, Don—" The innkeeper caught himself. "Perfectly. Follow me."

"Get the manzanilla. We'll wait."

The fat little man hurried out and Manuel examined Anna. Some of the effects of the liquor had worn off and she was a little worried but ashamed to show it. Spoiled and rich, he told himself again. He took the bottle from the man and followed him up the stairs, Anna beside him. At the door he pushed past the proprietor and kept him out of the room while Anna went in.

"That's all," he said, and shut the door.

She was standing in the middle of the room away from the big bed, her eyes cast down. Her hair had worked loose during the drive and wisps of it were straggling about her ears, pale in the dim light. Manuel put the bottle down and went to her and kissed her very hard. She was shaking in his arms, but soon she stopped shaking and began to breathe quickly. Her eyes were shut.

"Take off your dress," he said. "I do not want to tear it."

She did so, standing where she was in the middle of the room, not saying anything and beginning to shake again. When it was off, lying on the floor around her feet, he embraced her again. She felt smooth and slim in his arms and in the moment before all thinking slipped away he won-

67

dered how it was between her and Humboldt. Then he was far away, gone on a long and familiar journey to a place where there were no bulls and no horns and where nothing could touch him, where his strength was always limitless and the world was a good place.

Later there was the manzanilla, light and dry, and Anna was warm against him, quiet, thinking of Humboldt, he was sure. He felt better about everything now and almost liked her. She had got the rotten feeling out of him, and for that he was grateful to her. Paco, he thought, Paco made it happen this way, Paco with his puffed-up dignity. Now he could take his dignity and— And Gómez falling onto the horn. He chuckled to himself, thinking that Anna must have had a rotten feeling of her own.

"What's funny?" she asked.

"Everything," he said.

"Me?"

"You're very nice," he said. "Not a little bit funny."

"Don't try to say you love me," she said.

There it was, Manuel thought. They had to talk about it. That was the good thing about Mercedes. She liked it enough not to have to talk about it afterward.

"Drink some more of the manzanilla," he said. "It is good for what ails you, whatever it is."

"Where is this place?"

"Talavera."

"I'll have to tell all my friends about it," she said, looking away.

"This is where Joselito died."

"Here? In this roadside bagnio? I thought matadors were not at all like generals."

"In the bull ring," he said.

"That's better. It fits my ideas. Bullfighters should live in bed and die in the ring."

In the morning, in the bright sunlight that spilled across the bed from the small window set deep in the thick stone wall, she was just a woman who was in bed with him. Pretty, well formed, a little strange because she was foreign, but an object of contempt to him for yielding so readily. The small element of mystery that there had been about her, the holding back of part of herself even as she

68

gave herself to him during the night, had disappeared. He had breakfast sent up and then he was ready to be finished with it.

"Dress yourself," he told her. "I must return to Madrid."

"Now?" She glanced at her gown, lying on the floor. "It will seem a strange hour to be wearing that."

He shrugged his shoulders. "You can come later," he said, uninterested. "I will have it arranged so that a car will take you when it is dark."

She sat up. Her skin was very white in the sunlight and she stared at him without blinking, her blue eyes opened wide.

"Manolo, don't you want to stay?" Her voice was very quiet.

He made a brusque, chopping gesture with his hand, as he would at a recalcitrant bull. "What would I do here all day, woman? I have no desire to remain in this hotel room any longer."

She understood it now, fully. Her mouth went bitter, turning down at the corners, and she looked away out the window at the countryside that was already turning brown in the late-summer heat. She could see the dust lying in a thin haze over the fields and it seemed as though it were surrounding her also, drying her up, burying her.

"You've had your fun, is that it?"

"You're married, woman," he said irritably. "You have a husband."

"It's a fine time to think of him," she said.

"You think of him. I don't want to."

"Now I believe you," she said. "I really believe that you like the killing best."

Manuel didn't like the way that sounded.

"Don't talk about it so much. You wanted a *torero* and you've had one. You can go back to America and tell your friends how it is with a *torero*. You women are all alike. You think I am the bull. But a bull takes care of the herd and the cow doesn't cry after he's gone. There is no tragedy in this."

Charles would enjoy this, Anna thought. Oh, he'd enjoy so very much to be able to see this happen to her. His last words to her had come true very quickly and her confidence slipped away. She had done this kind of thing herself so often and now it was her turn to feel it. It would not have been so important, just a lesson learned, if it hadn't been that this was a man, a real one, not like the imitation heroes she had known.

She looked at Manuel, not seeing him as he was beside her, lean and hard-muscled, his indifference as hard as his body, but as she had seen him in the bull ring, graceful, moving with a slow and sinister arrogance that emphasized his power and domination. It was this same arrogance that was now thwarting her, dominating her. She could not accept his indifference as real and solid and she tried to push against it, forgetting about dignity.

"Can't I stay with you, Manolo? I wouldn't be in your way. I'd be good for you. We'd be good for each other."

He pulled away from her and got out of the bed, angry and contemptuous.

"You are ridiculous," he said. "What would I do with an American woman traveling with me to the *corridas?* You want to make me ridiculous? I am a matador and it is serious, not a joke."

She began to cry softly and it made him angrier.

"Besides, I already have a woman," he added.

She continued crying and he grew impatient. He picked up her gown and threw it on the bed.

"Dress yourself," he ordered. "I have had enough of this. I am not the first. Don't tell me that. Go back to that husband and ask his forgiveness. From that one you're sure to get it."

He began to dress, ignoring her, shutting the sound of her crying out of his mind. He felt stupid in the evening clothes now and was concerned about getting back to Madrid without attracting a crowd. Still crying, Anna began to dress. He was surprised at the tears. She looked tired and unlovely with her hair awry and the gown incongruous in the bare old room and the brilliant sunlight. Thinking of her accompanying him to the small provincial towns, he was struck with the complete absurdity of the idea, and he chuckled aloud. That made her stop crying to glare at him. Rich and poor were all alike when it came down to that, he thought.

When he paid the bill he warned the innkeeper again to

keep quiet, though he had no hope of that, only possibly to keep the American girl out of it. She began to cry again in the car and she kept it up all the way into the city. That she managed to stop easily enough shortly before arriving at her home made him smile. When he let her out she ran through the wrought-iron gates without a word or a backward look, heels tapping on the cement walk. He glanced casually at two men standing alongside the gate and drove off, not noticing them follow Anna through the gates toward the house.

His thoughts returned to his own life and he decided he would have to do something about Gómez. A contribution or something. Better yet, a benefit. Why should he shell out the money? Let the public do it. All proceeds to Tono Gómez and his family. That would stop the mouths. Fill them with pesetas and they would remain quiet.

Chapter Ten

The house was silent, seeming empty when he got home. The faint odor of food told him the cook was there, at any event, but the quiet made him feel lonely. Before the bulls that loneliness had been the ordinary thing, something normal as life, but now he was no longer used to it. He was accustomed to having people around him all the time, to being followed by crowds, by flatterers, women, and all kinds of hangers-on. Moments alone were rare things for him and he did not enjoy them when they came.

He liked this well-appointed house, not for itself but for the feeling of solidity it gave him. Bare rooms bothered him now and he liked to have carpets on the floors, pictures on the walls, and lots of furniture all around. In the arena the horns were always there to remind him that in an instant it could all disappear and among the crowds he could never forget their fickleness. But here everything was substantial, almost invulnerable.

Going upstairs he ripped off his tie, eager to be out of these clothes. He glanced into Mercedes' room, but it was empty and he wondered where she was. He found her in his bedroom lying on his bed wearing a green silk housecoat and nothing else. The rose-colored bedspread set off her swarthiness. She was not sleeping but lying on her back and staring at the ceiling. When he came into the room she did not turn her head or greet him in any way, her square heavy face brown and sullen. Her manner made Manuel pause. He studied her silently, seeing her body through the thin wrapper, knowing well its strength and its warmth, wanting it again, as always. He could not tell if she knew about Anna. He threw his jacket on a chair and caught sight of himself in a mirror and saw also that she had moved her gaze from the ceiling to him. His beard had grown out overnight and his long face was dark and shadowed. He went over to the bed and sat down beside her.

"And how is it with you today?" he asked quietly.

She had returned to staring at the ceiling and she did not reply. Only a tightening of the lips showed him that

72

she had reacted to his presence. Her silence irritated him, but he was careful to be gentle with her, not because he regretted what he had done—he didn't—but because she was the last of the beginning, all that was left of that day in Zaragoza.

He answered his own question: "I see it is not well."

She made a hissing sound without parting her lips, which were deep reddish brown without make-up. When she turned to look at him the brown eyes were almost hostile.

"It goes well with you, though," she said huskily. "It goes well and proudly, does it not?"

"Well enough," he said carefully.

She lurched heavily on the bed, turning to face him, and the silk wrapper fell open. His eyes went to her and she pulled the silk about her, the sullenness going out of her eyes and anger replacing it.

"And did the master sleep well?" she demanded ringingly. "Has he had enough?"

So she knew. It must be all over the city, he thought. It had started to spread the moment he stepped into the café and it had made its way like a wind-blown fire. A first-class subject for the mouths. He found the situation tiresome and he would have liked to walk out on it.

"Don't take on so," he said coolly. "She was just a woman, that's all. I felt like it. Don't play the innocent with me, because I've known you too long."

She squirmed around on the bed and got to her knees, shaking a fist at him, her mouth distorted with anger. Manuel made a vague movement with his hand as if to dismiss the whole affair, but Mercedes, thinking he was reaching for her, slapped his hand down sharply.

"Don't play around," she hissed.

He made a grating sound in his throat and stood up, black eyes hot now, his face darkening.

"Leave off, woman! Don't bother me with this stupidity. I am getting tired of this play-acting."

"I could stand much," Mercedes said. "I could stand Gómez and I could stand Paco. I could stand the dozens of tarts that there were along the way and the dozens of others who were not tarts but who flung themselves at you. This I knew when it began, and though it was some-

73

thing I could not like, it could be supported. But this stupidity with an American, this arrogance before the whole city—after Gómez and after Paco—this is too much. I have not the stomach for it and I will never have it, though mine is a strong stomach."

He felt the force of what she said and knew that there was justice in it. But he would not allow himself to be bound by these rules, to be limited by what others thought right or wrong. He accepted only the limits imposed by his own desires and his own strength. This was the way he had done it from the first and if he broke a rule, then it did not exist for him because it was he who had broken it and none other.

Yet he could not simply dismiss her, toss her aside, turn on his heel and walk away as from a slain bull. She was in him, of him, tied in a hundred ways to what he was and, more important, what he had been. While he had Mercedes he still had connection with the hungry, ambitious boy who had vaulted into the bull ring in quest of his destiny.

Gentleness, any form of weakness, was a stranger to him. If he had wanted to, he would not have known how to act in this manner. Besides, he did not need her for herself any longer. That he could replace easily enough and he knew it. But if having her for the other thing, for the mirror she held constantly before him, was important, it was not enough to make him yield any of his freedom.

"Your stomach is no concern of mine," he told her. "Take yourself and your stomach out until you calm yourself."

He turned his back on her and walked toward the closet, pulling off his jacket as he went. He was holding himself in check, not wanting to let his anger out on her, but she did not care, though she knew it, and bounded off the bed and ran barefoot across the room in front of him.

"I've had my fill," she shrilled. "My fill, you hear? It was not enough for you to humble me in my own eyes. It was not enough for you to take a man's woman from him. No, Manolo must do it in public, before the whole of Madrid. I will not have it any longer! Mercedes is not anyone's leaving, not even yours. I will not have them laughing at me in the cafés. It's too much and cannot be supported."

He pushed her away angrily. "And I've had my fill! Get out! Don't support it. Get out together with your stomach! I've had enough of your screaming and your complaints. You're not old enough to be my mother and not young enough for a wife."

She paled momentarily and they both fell silent, glaring at each other. It had gone further than either had expected and they were both remembering what had been before, searching for a sign of softness in the other, a hint that there was still something left. It did not come. She pulled the silk wrapper closer about her, a gesture chosen instinctively to remind him of what it scarcely concealed.

"Veneno warned me," she said as if to herself. "And he was right. Dust, all dust under your feet. You must humble and you must destroy. That is the way of Manolo. Veneno saw you clearly from the first."

"What you were you remain," Manuel said, his voice slashing at her. "But older now and growing older every day. *Puta*. Go back to the cafés and find yourself another sword. Perhaps another *fenómeno*. Or one that is eaten up with fear and needs an older woman to mother him and pity him so that he can nerve himself up for another day before the horns. Take yourself out, and with quickness, because I find that my stomach also has its limits."

"So it is finished at last," she said quietly. "I did not think it was forever. It does not hurt me that you call me old and I know it for what it is, a part of your cruelty, a part of your greatness. I am going and I would not stay any longer in any event. I am not one of those who plead and cling and wet their eyes with such stupidity. I think I knew it was finished when you told me that Paco had gone, but I stayed out of a woman's weakness and I have paid the price for the weakness.

"Yet I would not have done without this, for now I know, Manolo, and I can see the end clearly. I can leave content, sure that cruelty is repaid by cruelty. I will have my revenge, Manolo. Do you know what it is? Do you perhaps fear it even now in the days of your greatness and your strength? The horns will bring my revenge, Manolo."

He interrupted her with a laugh.

"You laugh," she continued, "and that too is like you. No one should laugh at death. You are not the bull and you will discover pain someday. You will die badly, Manolo. On the horns, torn, smashed, bloody, the arrogance and the pride destroyed even as you destroy, completely and without pity. I shall be there to see it. You will know the day of your death when you see me in a *barrera* seat."

She went out quickly without waiting to see if he would reply. Shaken a little, more by her manner than by her words, he absently rapped his knuckles against the footboard of the bed and then, catching himself in the superstitious gesture, he cursed himself loudly. He heard her moving in her room, pulling out drawers, slamming things around, and he shut his door.

He was alone. He felt it as a physical thing. It was not like the other lonelinesses he knew. It was not like the loneliness that wrapped itself around him when he went in to kill, that walled him off from the thousands of onlookers, that was an intimate thing between him and the bull. That was a loneliness that ended with the sword thrust, destroyed by his skill and strength, conquered, shed, forced to pass from him to the bull.

This was different from that. It was different also from the loneliness of poverty, which he knew well. There was a comradeship in that loneliness that defeated it because there were many poor, and a glance up the street told you that you were not really alone. This loneliness that he felt now was a new thing, the loneliness of being surrounded by people to whom he meant nothing, to whom his death would mean only the loss of income.

Death. Here was the heart of the matter. Death was a lonely thing and he looked at it squarely for the first time since he had become a matador. Mercedes had spread it out before him and he understood why he had hesitated to be rid of her, though he had tired of her some time ago. She was his tie with life, a means of defeating the loneliness of death. If the horns had found him, some of himself would have remained alive with Mercedes. Now he had thrown that away.

He shrugged it off, making the physical gesture contemptuously. He was not afraid of death and he was proud that he could say it truly. As it had been before, so it would be now.

He got up and went across the corridor to her room. She had gone already, leaving her things packed in two suitcases standing on the floor. The room was filled with her scent but it did not move him at all. He had never been in her room before; she had always come to him. He lifted one of the suitcases to the bed and opened it. Reaching into his pocket, he took out his billfold. He slipped out all the money in it and laid it on top of the pile of clothes. Then he closed the bag and went out.

Chapter Eleven

It had grown dark and he was still alone when he heard the doorbell ring. Wondering who it was, he listened for Elena to waddle out of the kitchen to answer the ring. The footsteps were heavy. Two men, he decided. They came up the stairs toward his room and he reached out and flickered on a bed lamp. Two Army officers in dress uniform came into the room.

Manuel blinked at them and sat up, swinging his feet over the side of the bed. He gestured at the chairs without speaking and went to the door.

"Elena," he shouted, "some wine."

"It's not necessary," said one of the officers.

Manuel could not guess their rank from their insignia.

"A benefit for the wounded?" he asked lightly.

"Captain Domingo Ordóñez," said the taller of the two men. "My colleague is Captain Jesús Sanjurjo."

"A pleasure," said Manuel, wondering. "What can I do that will be of service to you?"

The commandant of the garrison wanted tickets for the next *corrida,* he thought, and sent two captains for a dozen tickets. Or maybe he had a nephew who wanted to be a *torero.*

"I have orders to ask you to accompany us at once," Captain Ordóñez said stiffly, remaining standing.

Manuel came to his feet. "What's this all about?" he demanded.

Elena came in with a bottle and glasses on a tray, which she set down on a table. He waited for her to go out and then poured the wine, offering it to them. They took the glasses but did not drink at all. Their attitude made it seem quite serious.

"I am not at liberty to explain anything," Captain Ordóñez said. "My orders are to bring you back with me immediately."

"I am under arrest?" Manuel asked, puzzled.

The captain shook his head. "No. No arrest. Just that you are to go with me."

"And if I am busy?" Manuel smiled coldly.

78

"Then you are to come anyway," the captain said flatly.

Manuel nodded. "It is a real mystery," he said. "Where do you take me?"

The captain remained silent, looking uncomfortable. The other officer, who had not spoken, was looking at his wine. Manuel raised his glass in a mock toast.

"Well, let's drink to the success of your mission. I'm not busy at all."

They drank very seriously and Manuel laughed.

"I'll go," he said, "but I won't shave."

They waited while he dressed. Then they left, an officer on each side of him. A big black official car was standing outside Manuel's house with a soldier at the wheel. In the car the officers sat silent on each side of him, staring straight ahead. The car moved swiftly through the traffic and pulled up before a large modern building, in which most of the windows were dark. Manuel guessed it to be a government building. It surely was not a social affair.

Their heels rapped on the linoleum-covered floor, which was waxed to a dull shine, and Manuel was conducted through a series of empty outer offices to a glass-paneled door. Captain Ordóñez knocked once and then pushed open the door without waiting for a reply. A slim light-skinned man was seated at a large desk, clear of papers, and he looked up as they came in. His face showed nothing. He nodded at the officers and at Manuel.

"Leave us," he said to the officers.

They clicked their heels, saluted, and went out, closing the door behind them. The man behind the desk waited silently as their footsteps receded. When he could no longer hear them he raised his head and examined Manuel. Manuel turned away from him, took a chair, and pulled it up to the desk, irritated now at all this mystery. He sat down facing the man, scowling.

"With your permission," he said.

The other's eyebrows went up at his sarcasm.

"You are Manuel Ortega, called Manolo," he said in an official voice.

Manuel made a snorting noise.

"This is serious," the man said.

"It is a comedy," Manuel said. "A fancy comedy with all the trimmings. But already it is beginning to bore me.

Make it quick, because I do not have the whole night to waste."

"Do you know where you are?" the man asked.

"No. Nor who you are. If anyone."

"This is the Ministry of Foreign Affairs."

Manuel leaned back, smiling. A foreign tour. It was a funny way for them to go about it, but he supposed they did not want the publicity. He waited for the man to continue.

"I am Ramón Samayoa y Fraga, assistant minister. Manolo, you are an important man in Spain. To our people you are a hero. To the foreign world you are one of the symbols of Spain, a figure of magnetism and allure."

Manuel waved an impatient hand in front of the diplomat. "I know, I know," he said.

"Last night," Samayoa continued slowly, "you were a guest of the Marqués de Villaverde. Is that correct?" When Manuel nodded, he resumed. "You went to a café with the Marqués and an American couple, Charles and Anna Humboldt. And after?"

That kind of foreign affair, Manuel thought. He grinned again.

"I did not think the government was interested," he said.

"Do you know who Humboldt was?"

Manuel shook his head. It was beginning to look serious now. Humboldt was somebody important.

"A member of the American Legation here," Samayoa said.

Now Manuel thought he had it. Another diplomat. Another member of the club. But it still didn't make sense.

"So?" he asked.

"You went off with Mrs. Humboldt, is that right?"

"I don't like this." Manuel got up and leaned over the desk toward Samayoa. "That's my business. Tell Humboldt I am not interested in his wife, if that's what's bothering him."

"You tell him," Samayoa snapped. "He's dead."

Manuel recoiled from the desk. "How?"

Samayoa studied him, expressionless, his eyes cold. "The police have told me it was suicide."

"A bullet in the brain?"

Samayoa shrugged. "Perhaps yes and perhaps no," he said. "A delicate matter. And you are involved."

Manuel paced the room. He did not like this at all. It was all happening a little too fast for him. Gómez, then Paco, then Mercedes, and now this. He could not hide from himself and he knew that in some measure he was responsible. Had Anna killed him? He could only guess. He reminded himself that Samayoa was watching.

"What do you mean, I am involved?" he demanded. "A man kills himself. What is that to me? Or to you and the government? Many do this."

Samayoa's smile was thin-lipped and Manuel got the impression that he was enjoying himself.

"It is all over Madrid that you were with his wife the night it happened. After all, you do not think that we followed you. A walk into any café and we have all the information we need. All? Too much. More than we want. You understand, Manolo, more information than is good in such a case."

"It is not a case, it is a suicide," Manuel said loudly. "You're talking in circles and I'm getting dizzy following you."

"I'll make it simple for you," Samayoa said. Manuel could have hit him for his disdain. "Humboldt was a diplomat, not important in himself, but a diplomat and the son of an important father. The woman, the beautiful Mrs. Humboldt, a cipher, a butterfly, but the daughter of a very rich man. You begin to understand?"

Manuel shook his head, though the picture was coming clearer.

"The American government is very important to Spain at this time. That is enough for you to know. Very important. Also important to Spain is the tourist trade, of which the American is the most important because it is the most wealthy. Simple thus far. At this point Manolo, first matador of Spain enters. A foreign woman, beautiful; a matador, young and handsome—the result is perhaps inevitable. But for Spain the result can be a disaster. You understand that, a disaster."

Manuel snorted. "What is all this nonsense to do with

me? All right. I spent the night with her. Then I sent her back to her husband and he put a bullet in his head. Or she did. It is nothing to me."

"It is not the kind of publicity the government wants about Spain at this time. Not in America. You understand publicity well enough. Well, that is the matter and that is what this has to do with you. You cannot have this becoming public. It is bad for our national interest and it is bad for the tourist trade. However, because you are Manolo and a hero to our people, the government has decided to intervene, to protect you from the results of your own folly. We will see to it that nothing is published in the press connecting you with the affair. We will conceal your role. We have delayed publication of the story for twenty-four hours, but we can hold it up no longer."

"Thanks," Manuel said nastily. "For this you brought me here with all this mystery? No wonder the government is always short of money."

"Watch your mouth. Even horses can go to prison."

"I've already been there," Manuel snapped. "I got my start in prison."

Samayoa got up and came around the desk. "In return for protecting you from this adverse publicity, the government has one request to make of you, Manolo."

"Aha, here comes the bull with the splintered horn," said Manuel.

"You are to leave the arena immediately," Samayoa said. "All contracts canceled. No more appearances this year, here or in the provinces. Not even abroad. You are to retire from the scene for six months, completely out of the public eye."

"What! Are you crazy, man? I have contracts all over the country, in France, in Africa. It is almost a million pesetas in contracts. Thanks for nothing. I will accept the publicity and I will accept the danger."

Samayoa rapped on the desk with his knuckles, his mouth going grim. "I have heard of your arrogance, but you are not dealing with cattle now." The bureaucrat had disappeared suddenly and in his place was an angry and impatient man. "You have harmed Spain, endangered the government's policy. Clear? The incident cannot be glossed over if you parade yourself in the plazas. And it must be glossed over. Do you think I had you brought here at night by two of the best officers in Spain to make you feel important? Your career as a matador is the smallest element in this situation.

"Now. You will notify all promoters that you are unable to fulfill your remaining contracts for the season. You will disperse your *cuadrilla* and you will leave Madrid and remain in the country, seeing no one, for six months. You have forty-eight hours to do this."

"I won't do it," Manuel said angrily. "I lose a million in contracts this season. Perhaps another million in contracts for the next season. It can finish me. It is September now and if I remain away until March it might be that I will not fight all next year in the main plazas."

"You leave us no choice, Manolo. The government would have preferred to have your co-operation, but if it cannot have it, then it will act in any event. No promoter in Spain will fulfill his contracts with you this season and none will book you for the next season."

"I have the contracts," Manuel said. "Don't try to bluff me. I can get every peseta."

"The promoters all have violations in the arenas," said Samayoa slowly. "They will all be discovered on the day of your appearances and the plazas will be closed."

Manuel whistled through his teeth softly. He could have run Samayoa through with his sword at this moment. He waved his hand wearily and sat down.

"And if I sue . . ."

"Exactly," said Samayoa. "Even if you won—and you sue before our judges—you would be finished in every plaza in Spain and Africa." He rubbed his hands together and smiled thinly at Manuel. "I thought we would finally reach agreement."

He studied Manuel for a moment and then resumed, a diplomat again.

"Don't think that the government has not considered your career in this matter, Manolo. It is precious to us and it is with great regret that we have taken this step. We understand the financial sacrifice you are making for your country and the greater sacrifice in absenting yourself from the arena. You have suffered wounds three times, is that right?"

Manuel nodded. He was on the horns now, all right. He cursed out loud and Samayoa watched him with some amusement.

"Your retirement will be announced to the press as being caused by adhesions resulting from the earlier wounds. If you handle it discreetly, Manolo, I suspect that your return can be made important enough so that you can recoup whatever losses you may sustain."

"You've thought of everything," Manuel said bitterly. "But what of my boys? I can't just tell them they're through. And without the income from the contracts I can't pay them."

"As you say, we have thought of everything. The *cuadrilla* will be paid exactly what it would have earned had all the contracts been fulfilled."

Manuel thought of something. "And what of Veneno?"

Samayoa smiled. "Our information is that there is no great affection between you. We have not considered it necessary to pay Veneno his percentage."

"At least that," Manuel said.

"You will stay at the ranch of the Duke of Valladolid. The Duke, who has been persuaded of the advisability of co-operating with the Ministry, has agreed to place his establishment in the country at your service for the six-month period at no cost to you. The Duke himself will remain in his city residence."

"All the trimmings, is that it?"

"You are an important man, Manolo."

Manuel got up. "Anything else?"

"You are to tell no one of this. No one. Not even your *cuadrilla*. And you are to leave Wednesday."

"The mouths will have plenty to talk about then."

Samayoa slapped him on the back. "Don't be bitter, Manolo. The six months will pass quickly enough. And if you co-operate, perhaps the government will help make your return a triumphant one."

"I have no need of the government for triumphs."

Samayoa smiled once more. "Tell me something, Manolo. The American woman, was she worth it?"

Manuel swore. "A million pesetas! Is there such a woman in the world?"

"An expensive night," Samayoa agreed.

"I'll be loyal to our Spanish women in the future."
Manuel's smile was wry. "I have at last discovered the joys
of patriotism."

"Wednesday, then. An Army car will come for you."

Manuel went out through the dark offices. Up front the
two captains were waiting for him and fell into step on
either side of him without speaking. He had indeed fallen
into the horns, Manuel thought.

Chapter Twelve

Like a dream repeating itself in life, everything that had happened between Mercedes and Manuel had been known to her beforehand. At each stage in the relationship the pattern had made itself felt in advance—love, triumph, and final rejection—yet she had been unable to tear herself out of it, weakly playing out her assigned role. The beginning had forecast the end.

Now she hated herself and she hated Manuel. She hated herself for being weak, for waiting for the blow to fall, for being stupid and defenseless. She hated him for being cruel. For two days she stayed away from the cafés, remaining in the room she rented for herself, nursing her hate and hiding from the scorn she was certain would greet her if she showed herself. She needed the money that he had put in her bag and that made her hate stronger, because he had been able to make this gesture at the expense of her pride.

On the third day the papers told of Manuel's "injury" requiring his indefinite retirement from the plaza. The news thrust her out of the state of helplessness into which she had fallen and roused her to activity. That the injury was a fiction Mercedes was certain, but what lay behind it she could not guess. Of only one thing could she be sure—that Manuel had been forced into this step unwillingly. She knew what it must cost him in contracts, and the thought that there was someone stronger than he brought vague thoughts of vengeance to the surface of her mind.

The Café Sánchez was on a side street off the Puerta del Sol and it was a rare tourist who ever found his way into it. It was a café where *toreros* went when they wanted privacy and a chance to chat with one of their own kind without being interrupted. It was fancied by the first-class *banderilleros* and picadors who did not have to hang around the other cafés in the hope of picking up a job here and there.

It was here that Mercedes went in search of information. Old Mama Sánchez had a warm spot in her for

86

Mercedes and she came bouncing out of the kitchen to greet her, drying her hands on a big white apron.

"Well, so your meal ticket has left you," she said, wagging her head.

"The same old Dolores," Mercedes said.

"*Toreros!* They're all the same. You're well rid of that one. Why don't you get yourself a steady man like mine? It's a better life than chasing after these heroes."

"I'm not so old that I have to settle down."

"And not so young that you can't think about it, my dear."

"Even from you I don't want to hear that. What do you hear about the news?"

"You're asking me? I expected to get some choice bits from you. I said to myself when Sánchez said you were here, 'Aha, now I'll find out about this mystery.' "

"I'm three days gone from the nest. It must have happened after our quarrel."

Mama Sánchez wagged her head toward the entrance. "Here is another friend of yours."

She got up quickly. Turning, Mercedes saw Veneno. He saw her at the same moment. They had not seen each other since that day in Zaragoza and she saw that he had grown heavier and was losing his hair rapidly. For a moment he stared at her, coming to a stop, and then he smiled widely and he came toward her table. Mama Sánchez bustled off toward the kitchen. Veneno came up to her, smiling all the time, enjoying this moment.

"So your time has come," he said quietly.

"Hello, Dion," she said indifferently. "It is three years since we have met."

"I warned you," he said.

She shrugged her shoulders. "Did you think I didn't know it? That is the difference between us. Sit down if you wish."

He hesitated momentarily, then sat down. She watched him with an air of indifference, knowing his shrewdness and that he had hopes of some gain if he bothered with her.

"I am not now thinking of money," he reassured her. "This is for pleasure."

87

"If this gives you pleasure, I can think of a greater one. It would be a thing we would enjoy together."

"It will come," he said smoothly.

"You are able to wait?"

"I am always able to wait. I am rich, so I can wait."

"You did not come here this morning to find me, Dion. You are expecting someone?"

He shook his head. "I came for the same reason you did."

"Then you know nothing."

"As little as you, though I had a small hope when I saw you."

"He had a lot of contracts."

"A million. He would not throw it away without reason."

"This of the old wounds is nonsense," Mercedes said. "They were nothing. They never bothered him."

"He has not taken the *cuadrilla,* but they will be paid."

She nodded slowly, an idea beginning to form.

"I hate him, Dion. He is great and I would not deny it, but this that makes him great also makes him hateful. I would like to see him destroyed."

He laughed, shaking his head from side to side. "You are incurably sentimental," he told her.

"You have no love for him yourself."

"And what is that? A feeling, nothing more. You want to destroy him? Then do it. Take a weapon and do the job. But don't expect me to join in this foolishness."

"Who was speaking of that?" she asked irritably.

"Then what?"

"In the arena."

"That is what I wait for. My only fear is that I will not be present when it happens."

"Then we are agreed?"

"In the hope," he said carefully. "But he has retired from the arena now."

"For a time. It was something forced upon him, of this I am certain. He would not throw away the money."

His eyes showed respect for her now. "I begin to understand you," he said.

"He must return," she explained. "Next year, not later. He must return in the spring. What have you heard from those with his contracts?"

Veneno smiled. "You are more clever than when I had you."

"You never had me."

"It is just an expression." Veneno never quarreled needlessly. "I had not thought of this, though I would have, I am sure. The promoters are remarkably docile about the breach of contracts and I do not understand it."

"But they do not like it?"

"I'm sure of that, though they have not showed it."

"Then let him return for nothing!" Her voice rasped with a sudden access of hatred. "Let all the contracts be filled without him. You can arrange this, Dion."

He nodded. "But what of your revenge, woman? This is my revenge, not yours."

"It is a beginning. The rest will come."

He got up. "I will help you in this gladly. And anything else of which you may think. You can depend on it, Mercedes."

She nodded, her interest in him waning already. She felt better for having taken this step, for having freed herself from the shadow of Manuel's domination. But, as Veneno had said, this was nothing much to her. What she wanted was his physical destruction. The sight of blood, Manuel's blood, and nothing less would satisfy her. How she could achieve that still baffled her. She could be pleased at having enlisted Veneno's aid in her mission, but she could not be proud of it. His pleasure at her situation rankled too much.

She went out of the café, walking slowly in the bright sunlight of Madrid, unable to enjoy the familiar sights where almost half her life had been spent. She remembered when she had first seen these streets with the rubble still in them, the buildings scarred and pitted by shellfire, windows still empty of glass, and the people, crushed by three years of siege, unable to take pleasure from the sudden end of battle.

It was a long time and she could not remember the girl of seventeen she had been then or the men who had made her a woman very quickly. The body was the same, perhaps a trifle heavier all around, but what was inside had all been changed by men and time. She did not miss the girl of seventeen, considering her a simple little fool, but she would have liked to have, at least for another short spell, her eager zest to live life fully. It was lost and Mercedes could not deceive herself into believing that it would ever again be found.

A poster advertising a *novillero* for this afternoon caught her eye. Victor Gómez. She stopped, staring at the poster, feeling the growing sense of a pattern emerging suddenly, curiously, as though it had been fathered by the very intensity of her wishes. An unusual excitement caught her and she felt momentarily lighthearted, swept up by an instant certitude that the instrument of her vengeance was at hand.

She knew the name, and seeing it on the poster now, Mercedes was struck by the same sense of predestiny that had shadowed her affair with Manuel. Victor Gómez was the younger brother to Tono Gómez, the matador who had been so gravely gored on Sunday, a *novillero* who had been working in the provinces overshadowed by his brother's rise to fame. His reputation was good and a big future was predicted for him by those who had seen him in action.

Getting a *barrera* seat proved no problem. When he took his position in the *callejón* Mercedes saw that he was a husky, well-proportioned young fighter with a big nose and short, thick neck, not so tall as Manuel and not with the same grace of movement. Mercedes told herself that one could not tell by his looks, but she could not swallow the feeling of disappointment she experienced.

In action he was better than she had expected, good enough, she thought, to be a full matador. There was nothing wrong with his bravery or with his confidence, and while he did not give the feeling of domination, of complete and cold mastery that Manuel gave, no one else did either and it could not be counted against him. She saw with satisfaction that he worked close to the horns, not stupidly, but with confidence safely grounded in good technique, that his capework was

90

sound though uninspired, and that he did not shrink from the killing, though again he did not bring to it the same utter dedication to the mystery of death that Manuel did. But all the rest could be learned, Mercedes knew. She was satisfied that her sense of fate had not played her false.

She knew the café he would choose to celebrate his small triumph, knew it exactly, though she did not know him at all or his friends or whether he had a girl or not. None of these things mattered, because his choice of a café was dictated by none of these things, but by the fact that he was a provincial and that he had made his first success in Madrid. And if he had a girl, that would not matter either, because the weight of Madrid had been thrown into the scales and everything that had been normal and routine up to now would be crazily out of balance.

It was a café frequented by the in-between of the profession and the established ones of the profession avoided it studiously because they could not bear to see what they had been or what they would become in the general run of its patrons. There were two kinds: up-and-coming youngsters like Gómez, rough, some boastful and others wide-eyed, eager, full of the knowledge of their strength; and, on the other hand, those who had begun to slip. These were the worst, though the established matadors thought the youngsters were harder to take.

The older ones, those slipping downhill fast, dominated those in attendance this night, and it was an ugly thing to see them stare resentfully at young Gómez when he came in, telling themselves that he never saw the day when he could carry their swords, breaking out in a cold sweat even as they thought it, the fear and anguish rising in them at the very reminder of the horns that had destroyed their bodies, their honor, their entire lives. Mercedes saw them when she arrived, but her eyes were not for them and she swept past them without a thought, recognizing several but not showing it. As she had planned, Victor Gómez was already there, seated at a round table with several older men, two bottles on the table. He was smoking a black cigar and his black hat was tilted back on his head and he looked very much the bumpkin trying to appear cosmopolitan. Mercedes had to remind herself firmly that her purposes were more urgent than lighthearted love.

She knew how she appeared in his eyes. He saw no plain, heavy brown face, and though he saw the difference in age, it did not diminish his interest. He saw Madrid in her, just as Manuel had, and all the other things that the capital meant to him. She was the pleasure of success, the spoils most readily seized, desirable for herself and also for what she symbolized to him. The one added bit of information that would dissolve his last hesitations—that she had been the mistress of Manolo—was even as she seated herself being whispered to him by one of the cronies at the table. It was too easy for her and Mercedes would have abandoned it at this moment because she demanded more of a man than that he be just a meal ticket and the thought of an affair with this totally undistinguished rustic was too much of a comedown for her. It was her other purpose, the opposite of love, that held her fixed on her course.

Almost to the moment that he rose and came slowly toward her she could read his thoughts, could gauge the growth of his desire by the number of times some of his coterie glanced toward her table in the back. He was just a little drunk, she saw when he stood over her table, silent while he thought up the words he did not need. She made it easy for him.

"Don't stand there blinking, young one," she said. "If you wish to talk and drink some wine, sit down. And do it quickly or I shall lose patience."

It was hard not to smile at the naïve pride.

He sat down. "Gómez," he said. "Victor Gómez."

"I know," she said. "I saw you this afternoon."

He beamed and took a long puff on his cigar before gesturing grandly for the waiter.

"You liked what you saw?"

It was put in the form of a question but there was no answer sought.

"It is not often seen these days. I suppose you are not long for the *novilleros*."

The form of the words was flattery but it was the hidden goad to which he responded, the foolish vanity slipping out of his face and discontent replacing it.

"No, not long," he bragged emptily.

"You have arranged your *alternativa* to become a full matador?"

"I expect it," he evaded.

"It takes connections. Everything is connections these days, young one. How is it with your brother?"

"You know him?"

She shook her head. "I was there when it happened and it caused me much sadness."

He remembered who she was again and his face turned ugly. She forestalled his anger.

"It was more than I could bear," she said, "and I did not hide my feelings."

"So?" He was waiting to hear more.

"It had the form of an accident and the goring itself was an accident, but that is all that was accidental about it."

"That is how I heard it," he said heavily.

"You heard no lie."

His hand tightened around the neck of the bottle and the hate he did not bother to conceal was what she had been waiting to see.

"I would like to spend an afternoon in the plaza with that one," he said.

"It takes much man."

The slow hard smile told her that he was more than a bumpkin, that the true man showed in the arena and not in the café.

"But it is not impossible," she added. "It is something I too would give much to see."

There were no problems now and what had to be clear between them was clear and they did not spend much time at the table or with the wine, having need to seal their unspoken bargain in the time-honored way. He swaggered a little when they went out but Mercedes did not mind. She felt a little like swaggering herself.

Chapter Thirteen

The farewells had been brief. Just the boys of the cuadrilla all together in a long-faced group, not understanding it, not believing any of it, but too surprised to ask questions. It had happened too quickly for thought to intervene and the only thing that broke up the smoothness of the separation was the surprising—to Manuel—fact of their affection for him. It was not something he had expected and when he noticed a certain wetness in Luis' eyes he managed to slap him on the back and remind him that it was just six months and not forever.

So for the second time in three years he set out from Madrid in a car headed for a distant ranch and an unknown future. The silent Captain Ordóñez accompanied him and the big Hispano-Suiza was driven by an Army corporal. Manuel was not ready to accept the course of events as inevitable and he was still angry about what had happened. It was only when the silence in the car became oppressive that the nature of his farewell intruded on him.

No one. That was the thing that stood out above everything. It was a sobering fact and it told a lot about his life and the way he had lived it. This loneliness mingled with his anger and made him bitter. He was not the man to look into himself and find the reasons there, to blame himself, to regret his acts, to feel contrite or beat his breast. Rather did he turn to face the world, at bay, his confidence in his powers undiminished. He, Manolo, would yet find the way to bring them to his feet, to smash the walls around him.

They drove northwest through the night toward the mountains of León, where the Duke's estate lay. The moon rose, large and bright, and the countryside slipped by, bright silver mingled with black and silent shadows. Hills rose up against the sky, not sharp, but rounded like a woman's body, thrusting up gently from the earth. It grew cold as the time passed and their breath vaporized. No lights showed as the car sped along and only rarely did they pass another vehicle.

It was well after midnight when they arrived, pulling off the road onto a bumpy and narrow dirt path that led twistingly, between tall trees, to a massive stone house high on a hillside. A hound barked somewhere behind the house and was answered by another. Stiff, Manuel climbed from the car, looking around at the darkness. A light gleamed faintly through a deep-set window that was more like an embrasure in a fort. A heavy wooden door, massive, like the house, was pushed open and two men came out, one tall and gaunt, the other older, smaller, and fat. Behind the house the hills were high and formed a semicircular backdrop for it.

"I am Julio," said the taller of the two men, "at your orders."

"There are some bags in the trunk," Manuel said. "The captain will open it. Be careful of the basket with the capes and the other stuff."

He reached back into the car and took the swords himself.

The shorter man introduced himself as Carlos and led them into the house. Manuel could see the walls were almost two feet thick and that the door was covered with elaborate ironwork that must have dated back hundreds of years. Everything about the house at once impressed him with its age and its sense of permanence. Its very massiveness gave it the feeling of being rooted in the soil on which it stood, immovable, belonging there as much as the hills themselves. Inside the ceiling was high, very high, with huge ancient wooden beams thrust across it. To his right he could see the flickering light of a wood fire and he went to it directly.

Carlos went through a door and shortly afterward came out with a platter of cold meat, wine, and glasses, which he set on a long table that he pulled over toward the fire. Manuel and Captain Ordóñez went to it directly, but the corporal remained standing at the fire. Manuel noticed it and glanced at the captain, who was eating hungrily.

"The *cuadrilla* also gets hungry," he said to the officer.

He turned and beckoned to the corporal, who came

to the table. Captain Ordóñez stared angrily at Manuel but said nothing. The army man's caste feeling aroused Manuel's bitterness once more. He was one of those who had done this thing, those rich and well born to whom he would always be a bootblack from Málaga. The Humboldts and the Samayoas and the Ordóñezes of this world seemed all alike to him at this moment, enemies to be conquered, humbled, and forced to accept him. It was that which still had eluded him and he felt himself fortified in his determination to wrest it from them.

The gaunt Julio led him to his room, which was up a flight of wide stairs and in the corner of the house to the northwest. It reminded him of the room he had occupied at Don Eduardo's, the bed being of the same four-poster style. It had been a long time since then, yet he felt now the same restlessness that had beset him then, the same rage at the thought of being penned in a corner, at having his fate decided by others. He still sought what he had sought then, a thing without a name, but always luring him.

His irritation with his exile did not diminish by morning. The captain and the corporal were gone by the time he rose and the ranch was busy with itself and he had breakfast alone in a big room, served to him by a fat, white-aproned woman who did not speak to him. Outside the sun was bright and warm, something he could not tell when he was in the old house. In the daylight the building seemed just as strong and massive as it had been at night.

He found the practice ring quickly enough. It was off to the southern side of the building adjoining the corrals. The ring was of wood and there were several rows of seats circling it where the Duke and his guests could sit to see the show. While he was examining it a man in a wide-brimmed, flat-crowned hat, a short leather jacket, and leather chaps came up, walking with the unsteady steps of one who spent much time in the saddle. There was several days' growth of beard stubbling his face, which was deep brown and lined. He touched his hand to his hat and Manuel saw the tobacco stain on his fingers.

"Don Manuel," he said. "Francisco Portaleza, *mayoral* to the Duke, at your orders."

Manuel grinned at him. "So you are the one responsible for the ones with the long horns with the sharp points."

He felt more at ease with this man than with the other kind and his anger slipped away quickly.

"The horns carry death for some and riches for others," said Francisco Portaleza solemnly.

"And exile for me," said Manuel.

"We were given to understand that you were injured," said the *mayoral,* politely but curiously.

"There are all kinds of injuries," Manuel grinned. "Mine is of a special kind."

"Then you will wish to use the ring?"

Manuel nodded. "Regularly. I have to keep in condition or my retirement will last much longer than six months. But not now. Perhaps this afternoon I'll work with a cow or two. Just capes."

"At four o'clock," said Francisco. "I will have two cows ready and some men. Would you like a horse to ride about the ranch?"

"Many thanks, but for now I will walk."

The ranch was a vast affair, stretching for miles. Raising bulls was only one aspect of its life, though this dominated all else. Many families lived on the ranch, some working directly for the Duke, others working part-time and sharecropping small parcels of land. Wherever he went he could see them at work, the girls bare-armed, round, browned by the sun, the men lean and hard-looking, wearing stiff black trousers and rope-soled sandals. The girls looked nice to Manuel, reminding him of Málaga and the south and the times when a bull was a dream and not an enemy.

The boredom of a day spent alone was something Manuel had not reckoned with. By four o'clock he was eager for his practice session so as to have something to do. His temper was brittle now and the eventless day had made his rage at this exile return more strongly than it had been at his arrival. The thought of six months spent this way, alone, cut off from the only life he knew, seemed more than he would be able to stand.

97

He practiced in his ordinary clothes, just changing his shoes. Several ranch hands stood around with capes and Francisco ran the show. The cows were good and Manuel enjoyed working with them. He went through his entire repertoire, trying out new passes and taking pleasure from the *Olés* he evoked from the ranch hands. He was almost finished with the second cow and he led her across the ring in the *quite de la mariposa,* the butterfly pass, and reaching the planked fence, he finished off with an elaborate *serpentina,* the cape flowing out in a narrow, swirling, twisting band of scarlet, sending the confused animal away from him so that he could turn his back on her.

"Olé!"

He looked up quickly to where the girl's voice had come from. She was standing among the seats that girdled the top of the arena. She must have come in while he was working because he had not noticed her before. The sun was behind her, lighting her black hair brilliantly.

"Olé!" she said again, and clapped her hands.

He bowed to her. As he straightened his instincts warned him and he whirled in time to deflect the sudden charge of the cow with a flick of the cape. The ranch hands lured her out of the ring with their capes. Manuel looked up at the girl again. She was standing as before, but her face showed that the cow's sudden charge had frightened her and she had not yet recovered her composure.

"Save your *Olés* for something serious," he called.

"It was serious enough for me."

Her voice was high and clear and very pleasant to the ear. He stared up at her for a few moments longer, but the sun made it impossible to see her clearly and he turned to go out of the ring.

"Is that all?" she asked.

"Two is enough," he said brusquely. "I am paid only for two animals to a *corrida.*"

Laughing, she pulled a silver clasp from her hair and flipped it down into the arena. "I will pay for the next one," she said.

98

Manuel poked the clasp with his toe, his face turning harsh. The rage that had roiled in him ever since his arrival found its focus in the gleaming bit of silver lying in the dust before him. He picked the clasp out of the sand and tossed it up to her without looking at her.

"It's not enough," he said loudly.

From the way the ranch hands looked at him he guessed that she was more than just a girl, but he went out of the practice ring without a backward look. He jerked his head toward her and asked Francisco who she was.

"Teresa, daughter of the Duke," said the foreman.

She came down from the seats while he was standing there and Manuel saw that she was very beautiful. Her hair was deep black, parted cleanly in the middle and gathered simply at the back of her neck with the silver clasp she had thrown to him. Against the blackness of her hair her skin was very white, pale, unblemished, giving a feeling of coolness to all of her. Her eyes also were light, gray-green without a touch of hazel, large and under smooth brows that were black arched streaks against her paleness. Her nose was small and straight, and her mouth was full and red but without a hint of thickness.

She was wearing a white shirt open at the throat and tucked into tan jodhpurs that emphasized the narrowness of her waist and the womanly flare of her hips. Much woman, Manuel thought. He guessed her to be a few years younger than himself.

"Señorita Teresa," he said, "I am Manuel Ortega."

She nodded briefly. "The ranch of my father, the Duke, is honored at having the great swordsman of Spain as its guest."

He did not miss the mockery of her using the stilted old phrases, and if he had missed it, her eyes were eloquent enough. It was the clasp, he knew, and it brought a thin smile to his mouth. A duke's daughter, but a daughter nonetheless, like all other daughters.

"The swords will remained sheathed for the six months that I must stay here."

"Must?" Her eyebrows arched still higher.

99

"I have injuries and must rest for them."

She looked a little surprised. "I saw no sign of injuries," she said.

"It is not the greatest mystery in the world."

She turned toward the house and he walked with her, her beauty very much in his thoughts.

"Are you staying long?" he asked.

She looked at him coolly, estimating him, searching the question for its real meaning. Her mouth turned down at the corners, giving a fleeting impression of cruelty, and she shrugged her shoulders indifferently.

"I missed you at breakfast and lunch," she said. "Will I see you at dinner?"

"I hope you won't be wearing a mantilla."

Her laugh was bright and clear. "At dinner, then."

When he saw her then in a white dress with the black, black hair falling softly on it, his throat began to ache. It was like nothing he had ever felt before, except that day in Zaragoza when he went in to kill his second bull. It was as if all he had ever wanted was lying at hand, waiting to be seized, but the wanting was so good for itself alone that he could not move to end it. Even as he saw her he knew that she was completely aware of the effect she was having on him. She poured wine into two glasses and held one out to him.

"To what shall we drink, Manolo?"

"I prefer Manuel," he said.

She held up her glass, waiting.

"To the bulls," he said, "who are no respecters of rank."

"To the bulls in their strength," she echoed.

"It's a strange place to find the daughter of a duke," he said, "a bull ranch in the sierras."

"It is a strange place to find the first matador of Spain," she shot back, "recuperating from injuries. My instincts tell me that there is a woman involved."

He laughed. "Yes, it is because of a woman. Does it please you to know it?"

Her eyes mocked him. "I'm not displeased," she said.

He was suddenly irritated by this pointless verbal fencing. It reminded him of Samoyoa and the other

100

aristocrats who were always so surprised that he could speak with as much cleverness as they. He did not lose sight of her beauty, but for the time being it lost importance for him. She seemed to him to be representative of all those who had allowed him to come among them without accepting him.

"You don't belong here," he told her. "You belong in San Sebastián with all the others."

"Monte Carlo," she said. "I've just come from there."

"Then what made you come here?"

"I got tired of it. Sometimes it gets very tiresome."

"A man," he jeered.

"There are no men in Monte Carlo," she said.

"Such as they are, they are suited to their women."

He saw at once that he had mistaken her mettle. Her green eyes got angry very quickly and she stepped toward him, her chin up.

"That is twice that you have insulted me, señor," she said. "This is not a bull ring. It is my home, in case you have forgotten. What makes you so strong that you feel free to do it?"

He waved her anger aside with a laugh, pleased at having cracked her brittle poise.

"Sometimes I forget that I'm just a Málaga bootblack with good wrists."

"No bootblack ever had an arrogance like yours," she snapped. "They are pleased enough to get boots to black."

"I black no boots for anyone." He had anger to match hers and it came from a deeper fund. "Not for dukes and not for their daughters."

"No one asked you to," she said coldly, turning and going out of the room.

She went out like a duchess, Manuel thought. Or like himself after he had put a sword in a bull. Much style. A bootblack and a duchess. It was a thought that did much to restore the pride damaged by his exile.

Chapter Fourteen

As the days of his exile went by, his status made Manuel more and more bitter. To this bitterness was added the irritant that Teresa had cut herself off from him, haughtily refusing to speak to him on the rare occasions she allowed herself to see him. By the time a week had gone by Manuel no longer knew whether he wanted her for her beauty or for the revenge he could have on her and on the aristocracy that had formed her.

The fact that she was an aristocrat dominated his feelings about her. Up against the centuries that Teresa's family had been rich and powerful, his own climb to fame had no more substance than a shadow. To strike back through her at those who had exiled him from the bull ring was a desire that intensified steadily.

A late heat spell had come upon them and he was working in the practice ring one afternoon, wearing rope-soled sandals, hatless, sweating profusely, when he heard a shout of alarm from outside the ring. He sent the cow away with a toss of the cape and came quickly to Francisco, who was already moving toward the exit.

"What was that?"

"I fear a bull has got free in the patio," Francisco said, not pausing.

Manuel followed him quickly, carrying the cape over his shoulder. As they emerged he saw people scattering and off to the left a big black bull running free.

"Stay here," Francisco warned. "Wait for the men to come up with the horses."

As he said it Manuel saw a child who was running for safety stumble and fall, not fifty yards from the bull. The motion caught the bull's eye and he wheeled and came to a stop, looking for the child. Manuel started to run the moment the bull stopped, pulling the cape from his shoulder. He was farther from the child than the bull, but he had gained distance before the animal started his charge. The child, completely terrified, was unable to get up and run. A woman's shout of anguish came from the big house.

He had the situation figured out in bullfight terms, and as he ran he had already gauged the angle of the bull's charge and estimated where he had to intercept it to deflect it from the child. He was not thinking that this was not an arena and that he had a fresh, untired bull to deal with, but only of reaching the point that he had picked out. The sudden silence that fell over the patio was far away from him, as the noise of the crowd always was. When he was ten yards away he realized that he would not get there in time to take a proper position for a pass with the cape.

He flashed in front of the charging bull, which did not see him come, and neatly draped his cape over the animal's horns, blinding it. Tossing its head wildly to be rid of the cloth, the bull missed the child by more than a foot. Running quickly after it, Manuel snatched the cape from the horns and stopped, waiting for the bull to turn. He placed himself so that the angle of the bull's charge would take it away from the child. Out of the corner of his eye he saw Francisco moving cautiously toward them, making no sudden movement that might distract the bull.

"*Yaieee, toro!*" Manuel shouted loudly, stamping his foot and shaking out the cape.

The bull's tail went up and he charged viciously. As he went by Manuel punched him hard to make sure he would turn back to him. The bull wheeled quickly and Manuel passed him with a *recorte,* making him turn abruptly, wrenching his spine hard. Francisco dashed up to the child, picked it up, and ran toward the house. As Manuel set himself for the next charge he saw the horsemen come up with their long poles. The bull charged and one of the horsemen slipped his pole neatly between his hind legs and the bull went sprawling. Before he could recover, a rope looped around the hind legs tightened and held him.

Manuel walked away, wiping the sweat from his face with a corner of the cape. Francisco came out of the house, wide-eyed.

"I will never forget it," he said.

"It was just a bull, man," Manuel said.

"It was a child," said Francisco. "The bull was nothing. Never have I seen the like of it before."

The woman came out of the house with the child,

scolding it and kissing it. When she saw Manuel she ran to him and caught one of his hands and began to kiss it. Embarrassed, Manuel took his hand away.

"Here," he said to the boy, "take it for a memory."

He gave the boy his cape.

He saw Teresa standing at the door to the house and he made no attempt to greet her. She was watching him and then she came down and Manuel saw she was very pale.

"You had very great fortune that Manolo was here," she said to the woman.

He watched her, hard-eyed, saying nothing. She turned to him and they looked at each other in silence. She was clean and fresh, while he was in a sweaty shirt, his face still wet and streaked with dust, the black hair tousled and a day's growth of beard making his sun-darkened face even darker. For a moment her eyes held his and then her lids dipped down and a faint flush showed in her cheeks.

"That was a very brave thing that you did," she said softly. "Brave and noble."

"Fine words for a bootblack."

Her flush deepened. "I am trying to forget that, Manuel. I would like very much to forget it."

"It is forgotten," he said, smiling.

They were suddenly alone, the others having fallen away. The desire to humble her further slipped away and he allowed himself to enjoy her admiration.

"You're a hard man, Manuel. I've never met a harder one."

"The bull has no use for softness. He must be dominated."

"All things are not bulls."

"One dominates and the other yields. That is the way of life in all things."

"And who dominates the master?"

He did not miss the trickiness that had come into her eyes, and he chuckled.

"The mistress, of course."

"Then we can be friends," she said.

"Is it because you have no place to swim on all this ranch that you go to Monte Carlo? I'd like to find a closer place with this heat."

"There is a fine place."

104

"Then come with me tomorrow," he said.

"It's a long ride."

"I ride better than a picador."

"Agreed." She smiled. "In the morning when the dew is still wet and the sun is just topping the hills."

When he saw her the next morning in her shirt and jodhpurs with her riding boots polished to perfection, the old feeling came back and he could not swallow the sight of Francisco, a good man with an important job, standing humbly, holding the bay mare's head while she mounted gracefully into the saddle. The humbleness stirred the old resentments and made him wary of her purposes. He mounted his horse, a roan stallion, and looked beyond the house to the hills, where the mists were still to be seen against their shadowed slopes.

She set out at a slow canter and he followed along the road that led up from the house into the hills to the northwest. The pastures alongside the road were separated by broad belts of trees, which were already shedding their leaves. She slowed her pace, forcing him to come up beside her. To Manuel she seemed much subdued this morning, preoccupied and somewhat distant.

"Why did you leave Monte Carlo, Teresa?"

"It gets very flat sometimes," she said. "You don't risk life there, you waste it."

"What does a duke's daughter look for in life? She is born with everything already."

"I saw you twice in the bull ring," she said, "and I do not have what you have."

"Where?"

"In Madrid last year and in San Sebastián. It was very moving, but not like yesterday with the child."

"Yesterday was a spectacle. Death was very real."

"Death comes easily to your lips. Is it because you know it so well?"

"It's nothing to talk about," he said gruffly. "That's for the heroes of Monte Carlo. I speak of it because I live with it, but it holds no fascination for me. It is my enemy and I must know my enemy if I want to live."

"What is Monte Carlo to you that you scorn it so?" She was a little angry now. "I think you would like to change places with us. It is simple jealousy."

105

He did not see her as the kind of woman who would have much use for the weaklings of that set and some of the things she had said had seemed to tell him that, but now she was defending them nevertheless. In a curious way it affronted his manhood that she should stand up against his scorn for them and it meant only one thing to Manuel—that her identification with her own class was complete. She could be bored with them for a short while, she could find their effeteness offensive to her own strong and passionate nature, but she preferred them to one of his kind.

If she seemed to show an interest in him, Manuel was sure that it was just a diversion to her, something to revive her jaded tastes so that she could return to the placid upper-class life she led. He had felt the edge of condescension in Samayoa and it had been hard to take, but from Teresa it was impossible. The hate it roused in him demanded that he act to smash this subtle barrier between them, that he bend her pride to his own and force her to admit his superiority to the men of her own world. Yet he hesitated because he knew her to be different from the women he had known and he feared to appear ridiculous in his own eyes.

They rode on in silence, she leading the way up the mountain, past the last huts and out over broken ground on an indistinct trail. He watched her as she sat her mount, always erect, graceful in the saddle, sure of herself, and he knew that he would not break her easily. When they had been in the saddle for more than an hour she reined in her mount before a clump of trees at a level area not far from the summit.

"We leave the horses here," she said. "It's a short walk through the trees."

After a brief walk through deep shade they emerged on a flat and sandy shore overlooking a small mountain lake whose water gleamed bright blue in the hot sunlight. All around it the mountains rose steeply. There was not a sound except for the chittering of birds and the gentle rustle of leaves. Had it not been for the intensity of his preoccupation with Teresa, Manuel would have found the scene a marvel of serenity.

"Here I used to come when I wanted to be alone with

myself," Teresa said. "I would take out a pony and ride up the mountain and stay until close to sundown. It is a place with only good memories."

"There is only one place for me where the memories are all good ones and that is the bull ring at Zaragoza."

"I have never been here with anyone else."

It was something that she had said it and he realized it, but he could not overcome his wariness and he let the moment slide away. The pause lengthened and Teresa spoke again.

"What happened at Zaragoza?"

"My first," he said. "No triumph was ever so sweet."

"The first always seems the best," she said slowly, "but it is not really so."

Again he had the feeling that she was speaking of something else, that she was luring him with words he could not follow. He grew impatient with it and reached into the saddlebag for a bottle of wine.

"Put the bottle in the lake so that it will be cold," she said. "It won't take long. I am going to put on my bathing suit."

She went back along the path until she was out of sight, and while she was gone he slipped on his own trunks and lay on his back on the sandy shore waiting for her to return. With her out of his sight the turmoil fell away and he did not feel so much on his guard. He heard her coming back but did not turn to look at her. She spoke when she was very close to him.

"Now what do you think of Monte Carlo?" she said.

He sat up and turned to look at her, anger returning at her challenge. But she was not smiling and her eyes betrayed no malice and he knew that she was as beautiful as he could want a woman to be. He let his eyes feed on her until all anger and all hate vanished and the ache that was in his throat spread out until it filled all of him. He made a growling noise in his throat and, coming to his feet swiftly, he took the two strides that brought him before her and caught her to him.

As his mouth found hers he felt her resist and she managed to twist her head away and say, "No, no, no," before he smothered her protests. She fought him silently then but he was the stronger. The marvel of it was that when she stopped fighting him it was not a yielding, a passive surrender to his strength, but it was a passing over from one opposite to another, a frantic transition from resistance to ardor. He knew in that moment that she wanted his strength, needed it, as much as he wanted her loveliness.

With that knowledge there came to him an immense expansion of the spirit that lifted him out of time and place, that carried him beyond the sound of her voice murmuring his name and all sense of the world outside himself. For him now there was no sandy shore gritty beneath him and the hot sun that beat down on them did not exist.

Then, later, with her black hair spilling over his chest, she said, "Manuel, you are a man. All man, all man."

And it was good hearing her say it, knowing it to be true and feeling that nothing else mattered as long as that was so and she was with him to make it so. This then was what she had given him and he was grateful to her for it and proud silently to himself that he had taken it, that he had known it to be true all at once.

Chapter Fifteen

It was a different Manuel who returned to the ranch with Teresa, the memory of their love still warmly with him. And as the time went by and their affair deepened the change in him became more pronounced. It was as if the processes that had been at work within him since his start as a matador had been suddenly completed by the act of love.

Because it was love. There had been women before and he made no attempt to conceal it from Teresa. But now there was a woman. She filled a need greater than the physical, and the knowledge that he was loved for himself, for his simple qualities as a man, without thought of money, place, or prestige, affected him more profoundly than he realized.

For the first time in his life he had no hunger for attainment to spur him. It seemed to him now that he had achieved all he wanted, that with Teresa had come that last thing that had been lacking, full acceptance by the world.

With Teresa also came a sense of permanence. Manuel never analyzed himself, but accepted his feelings as truth. And since he now had this feeling of permanence he assumed it had come from Teresa and did not think of it as something that had come out of his own hunger for it. And, finally, having Teresa love him was a final conquest over the aristocrats. Now he had taken from them the best thing they had. He was, he thought, completely victorious and had triumphed over his exile.

In the rapid succession of days and nights they spent together he found Teresa a person much like himself. Though she seemed to yield to him dominance in the relationship, she was no weak woman and he was always conscious of her strength and independence. He would not have had it otherwise and it was just this strength of hers, combined with a passion that never failed to amaze him, that made him so proud to be her lover.

He furled his capes and sheathed his swords to plunge fully into this swift stream of love, abandoning himself to it. Thoughts of the bull ring slipped far from him as he and Teresa ranged the hills of her father's ranch, finding the quiet places where they could enjoy each other. It was a rustic idyll of love. If the people on the ranch noticed anything, they gave no sign of it, and there was not a cloud to mar the horizon that stretched before Manuel.

It went on this way for a month and as the days went by Manuel forgot that it could ever end. The end came abruptly with the first sprinkling of snow that greeted them one morning in the last week of October.

"This is no place to spend a winter," Teresa said, staring out the window of her room.

"You have wood and you have fires and you have food," he said carelessly. "What else do you need?"

"It is lonely and boring in the winter. You are penned in this house for days on end and there are few places on God's earth that are gloomier. Besides, it is always cold. My mother hated it."

"You won't be cold this winter," he said.

"Be serious, Manuel. The first snow is already on the ground."

"I am serious. Where would you go?"

He had never told her why he was on the ranch and she had never asked him and now he began to feel a little nervous that it might come up. He knew that he could not bring himself to admit this humiliation.

"The Mediterranean coast," she said. "It is warm there and the sea is lovely."

"You mean Monte Carlo."

She shrugged her shoulders. "Some other place will do, if the name offends you," she said carelessly. "The gambling does not interest me."

"I don't feel like traveling," he said with finality.

She did not press the subject and he assumed it was dead until she brought it up a week later.

"I think we must start to plan on leaving," she told him without any introduction. "I don't want to stay here another week."

"You find it dull?"

The ugliness that had crept into his voice did not intimidate her.

"The place, yes."

110

"Only the place?"

"Don't be ridiculous," she said irritably.

"I am never ridiculous."

She made the mistake of laughing at that and his anger flared quickly, for the first time since the beginning of their affair.

"I find this place fine," he said. "I think we will stay."

She picked up the challenge without hesitation, her green eyes glittering as angrily as his black ones.

"You think to dominate me?" she demanded. "I told you once I am no bull. You are unreasonable, completely unreasonable. Why must we stay here in the mountains with bulls and snow for company? What is so special about this ranch that we can go to no other? I don't want to stay and I won't."

She set her face stubbornly and he knew he was in for a battle, but he did not shrink from it. He could not justify his position and he would not explain, so he took refuge in similar stubbornness.

"I don't find the company dull here," he said tightly, "and I am content to remain."

She stamped her foot in irritation and paced the room.

"If not Monte Carlo, then another place," she said despairingly. "Choose it yourself, Manolo, because I don't want to stay."

"I have no other place, Teresa. I thought to stay the winter and resume my work with the animals to keep in condition for the season next year. Then in the spring we would return to Madrid and I would start killing bulls again."

She stared at him in disbelief. "You thought that? You thought we would stay here cuddling before a fire all winter? And then I was to follow you on a circuit of the plazas? What do you take me for, Manolo? You think I will follow a *torero* from plaza to plaza? Sometimes your arrogance is incredible. Put it out of your mind. I make no circuits with matadors."

His face turned deep red, and as the urge to violence caught him he pulled his lips back from his teeth and took a quick step toward her, then checked himself.

"You think yourself too good for a matador? You will make a circuit with some drunken seventh son of a seventh son from casino to casino in France, but a matador is not good enough for a duke's daughter. Well, I am no trophy for your beauty and you cannot dangle me before your useless friends in Monte Carlo. A matador lives in the arena, and if the smell is too strong for your noble stomach, that is too bad for your stomach. You will have to find yourself a milder dish."

She chewed on her underlip as he glared at her and, finally, turned away.

"I won't stay," she said. "I shall leave at the end of the week."

"Then go alone."

He walked out. He could not reconcile himself to the prospect that it was over and his yearning to heal the breach was great, but he was not one to put a collar on his pride. That she had taunted him about "circuits with matadors" festered in his mind and made his mood uglier as the day slipped into the night. Had it not been for that, he might have accommodated himself to her desire and left the ranch in defiance of the government.

She came to him when it was dark and flung herself into his arms without speaking and he took it for a sign of surrender. It spoke much for the depth of his love for her that he did not thrust her aside even at this moment.

"Manolo! I did not mean it as you thought," she whispered. "But did you really think that I could travel with you from plaza to plaza? You must see that it's impossible."

"I did not say it and I did not think it. I don't want to cause scandal for you."

"I'm not afraid of scandal, Manolo. I would glory in scandal about you and me."

"Your father?"

"I am his only living child and I can do no wrong for him. But I am not one to follow a *cuadrilla* and you would not want it so."

"And what of Monte Carlo?" he pressed.

"I cannot stay here all winter. You would find yourself going insane with boredom and it would spoil things for us. Do you think I want to hide away here with you? I want to be with you where all can see us together, so that the pride of it shall be mine as well as yours. I don't think

112

it a small thing that I want my friends to see you, that they should envy me for the man I have. Why can't you come with me, Manolo?"

She made it seem like a surrender, he realized, but it was the very opposite of that. She had taken him out from his defensive position step by step, using all her weapons, and he could not now return to where he had been.

"All right," he said amiably, "so I shall at last see this Monte Carlo. I don't expect much of it, because I think you have already shown me the best of what it has."

She laughed and he detected the note of triumph in it.

"You planned this before," he said.

"Of course," she said gaily. "A noble bull should not stay in the corral, but should head for the arena."

"Now it is I who am the bull." He grinned.

"Better than I, Manolo. You are a better bull than I."

"May I never wear the horns, though."

They left for Madrid at the end of the week after a second snowfall had almost blocked the roads. Manuel left his capes and other equipment behind because there would be no opportunity to practice where he was going. He told himself that he needed the rest and that he could condition himself quickly enough before the next season began, but he could not entirely suppress the small feeling of disquiet this step gave him.

Once on the road with Teresa, however, all such thoughts fled him. The promise of months of idleness and love proved too alluring. It seemed to Manuel that he had earned this after all the bitter years of doing without. He had reached the summit and it would be foolish to be there and not enjoy the glory of it.

Back in Madrid the city all seemed new to him, as though he were visiting it for the first time. He had been gone for longer periods than the six weeks that had elapsed, but now he saw it all more freshly. It was a fine thing to walk with Teresa through the city, to be recognized by the passers-by, to have to duck into a café to avoid the gathering of a crowd. It had always been an annoyance to him up to this time, but with Teresa there to see it, the fact of his fame was a sweetness as heady as an old wine. He had not forgotten the first time he had walked these same streets with a woman, the day Mercedes had bailed him out of jail.

Their plan had been to be discreet in Madrid, but Manuel was not now willing to have it this way. He was eager to be seen with Teresa and it was something that she also wanted, so they decided to go out together the one night they were to spend in the capital.

During the day, Manuel got hold of his boys. They met at one of the cafés and after the drinks and all the remarks at how well he was looking he took Luis aside and gave him the address where he would be staying in Monte Carlo.

"If anything comes up," he told him, "let me know."

"You are going to keep in trim?"

"What do I need? I won't forget what I know so quickly. I'll be ready for the next season. But remember, I'm depending on you to keep after Veneno."

"Don't worry about it, Manolo. Enjoy your retirement. The public is already waiting for you to return and the crowds will be bigger than ever."

Teresa was a revelation to Manuel that night. He had never seen her gowned, jeweled, art added to her beauty, and the effect was spectacular. Seeing her, he felt a little self-conscious. They chose a place that was public enough, but not too much so.

"I find you formidable tonight," he said.

"Nobody sees me. They have eyes only for Manolo. It has never happened to me before."

"I feel I should call you Duchess." He was smiling and the self-consciousness was going away.

"Don Manuel," she said.

They both laughed. Everything was suddenly flawless, the food, the popular ballads sung by a husky-voiced girl, the wine. There was an intoxication about it that caught them both, lifting them out of themselves, walling them from the world.

"This is happening to us," he said. "To no one else."

The bulls were far away and this smooth floor would never see blood. It was a triumph of triumphs and the horns had disappeared forever.

"There is a woman staring at you," Teresa said. "She is not beautiful, but I could fear her for a rival."

Manuel turned. It was Mercedes. He did not recognize the man she was with, but he had the look of a *torero*. He turned back quickly.

"Does she know you?"

Manuel nodded.

"Who is she?"

"She was part of the beginning," he said. "It was a long time ago."

"I think she hates you."

He shrugged his shoulders. The night was spoiled for him. "Maybe," he said.

"A matador's life is not all bulls," she said.

"No," he said. "Let's go."

Teresa looked at Mercedes again before she got up.

"She does hate you, Manuel. She makes me nervous."

"It's nothing," he said. "If she hates, it hurts only her. It was a long time ago."

He could not recapture the earlier mood when they left and he did not forget Mercedes until they were home and Teresa's beauty wiped everything out of his mind, the past and the present, leaving only the future.

They left for France and Monaco the following day, driving because they wanted the intimacy it gave them. It was cold, and when they reached the Pyrenees there were snow flurries and the day grew dark. Then they were at the customs and a few hours later the cold vanished and the sun was bright and warm and off to the right there was the very blue sea below the hills of the coast and winter had disappeared. The sky was cloudless.

Chapter Sixteen

Mercedes had made a mistake. It took her two more fights to realize that what she had seen Victor Gómez do in the Madrid bull ring had been an accident, a performance far superior to the present level of his talents. It was not that he could not improve, but that it would take so much time and so many gorings before he reached a point where her plan for revenge could be achieved that it was doubtful if it would ever come about. She was ready to abandon the whole idea, and Gómez with it, when she saw Manuel with Teresa at the night club.

The sight of him was enough to renew the hatred she felt, but the added fact of Teresa's beauty was a final drop of gall in her cup. That Manuel had reappeared on the scene meant only one thing to Mercedes: that Manuel's retirement would be shorter than she had been led to believe and that her entire scheme was in danger.

A question to the waiter brought her the information she sought. The value of the information did not reveal itself to her immediately, but when she added it to what she knew about Manuel and what she could guess about Teresa, the pieces fell into place, and what had seemed a forlorn hope a day earlier appeared ready of accomplishment today.

The secretary and the file clerk in the office where the Duke managed the affairs of his estate smiled at each other when the visitor appeared, and their eyebrows arched high. It was not what they expected of the old Duke, and even if it were just vanity, it could have been expected that he would be more discreet.

"I would like to see the Duke," Mercedes said.

"His Grace is busy," said the secretary. "What is it about?"

"It's personal," she said, smiling.

It had the effect she hoped for. While the Duke of Valladolid was not an easy man to reach—especially if one did not have an appointment—his secretary would not take it upon herself to deny access to this visitor. The risks were too obvious. The secretary went through an inner door and returned shortly afterward wearing a puzzled look. She motioned Mercedes through the door.

The Duke of Valladolid was taller than Mercedes had expected him to be, straighter than a man of his age should be, less forbidding than a man of his position could have been. His hair was white, but most of it was still covering his head. His eyes were alive, black and piercing; his nose was big, but not fleshy; the face was lined, though the flesh was firm and healthy-looking. One of the old kind, Mercedes decided.

"Señorita," he said, rising. "I think you shocked my secretary. Seeing you, I can see why. At my age I should be flattered."

He was, Mercedes thought, the kind of a man she could deal with. His big resonant baritone voice dissolved any nervousness she had felt on entering and she did not think of him as the Duke of Valladolid, but as a man.

"I have not come on matters of business," she said.

He indicated a chair beside his desk and held it for her while she sat and watched her when she crossed her legs, a faint smile on his lips. Like father, like daughter, Mercedes thought. It answered a question that had bothered her; she was certain there was no mother on the scene.

"Personal, my secretary said, Señorita . . ."

"Mercedes."

"A beautiful name."

"It is about Manolo, the *torero*," she said bluntly.

He seemed puzzled. "Why do you come to me?"

He was wondering if she knew Manuel was staying at his ranch, since it was supposed to be a secret. He had never liked the affair from the beginning, but members of the old aristocracy were in a difficult position under the present government, and it would have been more than foolish of him to refuse to co-operate in a matter that did, after all, cost him little.

"How many children have you, Your Grace?"

"One living."

"A daughter, very beautiful?"

"My daughter is in Monte Carlo," the Duke said.

Mercedes got up and paced slowly around the desk. "I

117

don't know where she was last week or where she is today, but last night she was in Madrid with Manolo."

"The devil you say!"

"I understand your feelings, Your Grace."

"You're sure of this?"

"You can check it yourself," she said easily.

He was under control of himself again, but she knew she had jolted him.

"What is your interest in this?" he demanded.

She shrugged her shoulders. "She is your only one. I think I can manage to smash up this affair for you."

"Affair? How do you know there is an affair?"

"I know Manolo."

He chewed on that for a minute. "How well?" he asked.

"I was his mistress from the beginning until September." She said it proudly.

"I see. You want him back."

"Never!" Her vehemence took him by surprise. "I want him dead!"

He got up and walked around the room, his steps muffled by the thick carpet. She watched him tensely, guessing at how deeply she had hurt him. It was not too deep, she decided. Nor was it entirely unexpected. The thing he did not like was the public aspect of it. He impressed Mercedes as a man who understood that his daughter had the same strong passions that he had and knew that he could not keep tight rein on her. But a matador, and a famous one like Manolo—that was something else. After all, he was still a duke. She felt certain that she had not misjudged the situation.

"I gather you have a plan, Señorita Mercedes," he said after a while.

"Then you believe I am right."

He waved his hand vaguely in the air. "If you're wrong, I'll know it," he said. "I would not like such an affair to continue. They are never good. And I would not like to intervene directly, since it would have only the opposite effect."

"I said I wanted him dead," she reminded him.

He snapped his fingers, carelessly. "I'm waiting for your plan."

"Good. I know Manolo and I know what he will do

118

now. He is ready for a rest from the bull ring and now is when he will take it. You mentioned Monte Carlo. That's where he will go. Let him go there and soften, get out of condition. That is the only way to deal with Manolo, in the ring. Let the bulls do the job for us."

"What do you want of me?"

"Money," she said. "Money and influence."

"For what?"

"There are many who hate Manolo. Some hate him enough to want to see him killed. One such is a *novillero* named Gómez. His brother was crippled two months ago because of Manolo's taunts. Another is his manager, Dionision Veneno. If we can keep Manolo out of the arena for the next season, we can arrange a special event in which he will meet the same fate as the elder Gómez. The *novillero* Gómez thirsts for revenge."

"Is he the man to do it?"

"He has the stomach for it and he has the wrists. That is why money is needed. Money to make a reputation for him, to bribe the critics, to provide him with a teacher to train him for the coming season and remove the crudities. In other words, to make him a fit rival for Manolo."

"If not?"

She shrugged her shoulders. "Then find your own way," she said.

He thought about it. "What if the affair ends quickly by itself?"

"Then you've wasted your money."

"I see. You are very direct. How do you know Manolo won't have contracts for the coming season?"

"I have Veneno's word."

His eyes gleamed and he smiled for the first time. "I like the sound of it," he said. "But Teresa must be kept out of the scene."

"She is a woman and beautiful. I cannot handle that."

He sat down wearily. "It's hard to be father and mother at the same time. God forgive me my failures." He looked up at her, the momentary weakness gone from his face. "We will do it your way," he said. "I do not hate him, but his life is less to me than my child's. I will pay for your revenge."

"He will not die so quickly," she said. "More likely he

will save himself and sacrifice his honor. It will be enough to achieve your end. I do not think your daughter will stay with a coward."

He nodded. "Then you will be cheated."

"It will be enough. You have not felt his arrogance. If that dies, Manolo dies with it."

"I have heard reports of it," the Duke said. He rose and walked with her to the door, stopping there, his eyes on her. "I will see you again, Señorita Mercedes?"

She smiled softly. "*Toreros* are notorious for jealousy," she said.

"And old men for foolishness."

"You seem not old to me, Your Grace."

"But foolish?"

She laughed. "My *torero* will be busy enough soon with lessons."

"Good. You see, I do not judge my daughter, but merely protect her."

She went out, amusing herself by waggling her hips to shock the plump secretary. Her revenge was nearer now and she could almost taste it, so sweet did it seem to her. If the daughter was like the father, Manuel would not be eager for the bull ring. She knew his taste for those pleasures well.

Another old one and her plan would be complete. This was her day of the old ones, Mercedes thought. She took a taxi and settled back, well pleased with herself.

Paco Torres lived in a modest rooming house that was home to half a dozen others, all associated with the world of the bull ring. His seamed face showed no surprise when he opened the door for Mercedes.

"You," he said, his pale eyes expressionless. "Come in."

"How have you been, old one?"

"Well enough. And yourself."

"I am not lonely."

"It was not to be expected that you would be."

"Paco! That is the first time you have ever complimented me. You must be growing younger."

She could not fluster him or penetrate his dignity. Nor could she bring a smile to his face.

"You didn't come here to ask of my health, Mercedes.

And I'm sure you're not searching for a lover."

"No. Not that. I'm not lacking for offers yet. I come on business."

"So?"

"I have a pupil for you. One who shows much promise."

"I will judge his promise myself. What is wrong with him? Is he lame that he can't come himself? Or mute?"

She laughed easily. "Neither lame nor mute. It is something that I do for him. I am a good judge of *toreros*, Paco."

"Spare me your boasting, woman. I know what you judge them for, and it is useless against a bull."

She flushed deeply. "Remember, it was I who discovered Manolo."

"I am too old to be impressed by your talents."

"Do not hide behind your years," she said. "Others older than you have more than memories. You were not so scornful in your youth, I have heard."

"Well, what of the pupil?" She could not affect his dignity.

"A *novillero*," she said, "with two years' experience and promising a long future. He will take the *alternativa* in the spring and there are crudities to be removed. I remember how you formed Manolo and I would like to have the same done with this one. He will pay the price."

"His name, woman. Doesn't this *fenómeno* have a name?"

"Gómez," she said.

He darted her a sharp look. "The younger one, the brother of him who was crippled?"

"The same."

"He has no money."

"I will pay it. He has much promise."

He snorted and turned away from her. When he faced her again his face was hard and hostile.

"I understand it now," he said slowly. "No, you are not stupid and this is not a matter of money or a lover or anything like that. I should have known it at once. Truly I am growing old."

"It happens to us all."

"Why did you choose me?" he demanded, coming directly in front of her. "I can understand it in you and it

121

is natural for you to do this. And the other, Gómez, I can understand it in him. But what made you think I would soil myself with that corruption? If I could not swallow Tono Gómez' blood—and it was not on my hands—why should you think I would put that on my soul now?"

"I don't know what you're talking about, old one. I offer you a pupil and you rave about your soul. You're older than I thought."

"Not for me! I will not play a part in this rottenness of a revenge. There is no love between Manolo and myself, but there is not blood and there will never be. Go to Chico Riúz or one of the others with your *novillero,* but leave me out of it."

"You're ridiculous," she said defensively. "You have a wild imagination."

"You betray yourself, woman. You have no cause to hate him. He treated you well and the end was to be expected. I will not be a part of this corruption. I have no stomach for it."

She got up, angry. Paco was as important as the Duke to her plan, but she would have to do without him.

"You and your stomach. Write a book with it. It sees things better than your brain."

She slammed the door on her way out, her good feelings gone and her guilt stirred by him. She remembered what she had said to Manuel after Tono Gómez and at the first church she came to she hurried in, knelt, and prayed hard for five minutes. Then she went out to search for Chico Rúiz, Paco's rival as a teacher.

III.

THE HORNS

Chapter Seventeen

Though it was March, the sun over Monaco was warm, and the small man with the sharp face, whose overcoat was too heavy for Monte Carlo and whose flat cap was too inelegant to pass unnoticed, was glad to walk out of the brightness into the shade of the ornate lobby. When he was inside he came to a halt and stared at the opulence around him, unconsciously rubbing his worn shoe over the thick carpet, his eyes trying to see the whole scene in terms of pesetas. He could only wag his head from side to side at the thought.

A bellhop came up and said something in French and the little man looked blank. He answered in Spanish.

"Where can I find Manuel Ortega?"

The bellhop showed him to the desk. The clerk there looked at him curiously and he repeated his question. The clerk looked as though he did not understand.

"Manolo. The matador. He gave me this address."

"Who are you?"

"Luis Vásquez, his sword-handler."

The clerk consulted with a bellhop in French.

"He's at the beach house now," he said to Luis. "The boy will direct you."

Luis felt out of place with the overcoat as he followed the bellhop out across a flagstone terrace. The elegant women made him more ill at ease and as he drew nearer the indoor swimming pool his face turned sullen and hostile. The heat of the glass-enclosed swimming pool combined with the moisture in the air made him sopping wet before he found Manuel. Despite his resentment he could not help staring at all the women, sprawled about in wisps of swimsuits. Manuel saw him first.

"Luis!"

The sword-handler turned at the call and saw Manuel

sitting beside the pool in a pair of trunks, his body tanned. A beautiful black-haired girl was sitting beside him and she said something to Manuel that Luis could not hear. It was in Spanish, however, and it made him feel a little better about the way things were. Manuel got to his feet and put out his hand.

"So I've got to get back to work already," Manuel said. "You didn't have to come yourself, man."

"You're looking fine, Manolo," Luis said. He didn't really think so. Manuel looked soft and out of condition. The gauntness was out of his face and he seemed to fit too perfectly into the indolent surroundings.

"A drink, man?" Manuel signaled and a waiter came over. "Some English whisky for my guest."

"I got the perfume you sent, Manolo," Luis said. "Many thanks, though my woman is no longer the same because of it. She wears it all the time, even to confession. The odor is becoming tiresome."

"If she wears it to confession, then it is all right."

They both paused and Luis felt uncomfortable.

"Well, when is my first fight?"

"That is why I came myself. There is none. Not one contract for the entire season."

"What!" Manuel caught Luis by the lapel. "You were supposed to keep after Veneno. What were you doing all this time?"

"Manolo, don't blame me. I'm only a sword-handler and I have no power over Veneno."

"Then why didn't you let me know before this?"

"Veneno fooled me. He kept telling me it was all being arranged. Two days ago he told me that there were no contracts. I left the same night. Do you think I find this good news?"

Manuel cursed heavily and Teresa got up and came over to him.

"Bad news, Manolo?"

Manuel continued cursing, keeping his voice low, his eyes alive and angry.

"I'm going back with you," Manuel told Luis. "Go up to my room and start packing my bags. I'll be right up. You're not too tired to travel?"

Luis grinned. "I bought a ticket for you at the station. The train is at ten o'clock."

Manuel slapped him on the back. "We'll teach those thieves. We'll let the public show them if they can freeze Manolo out of the arena."

Luis' face clouded.

"More bad news? What now?"

Luis glanced at Teresa and then back at Manuel.

"No, no more. That's all there is."

Manuel looked at him suspiciously and then watched him go off.

"What is it; Manuel?" Teresa asked.

"They froze me out," he said. "Not one contract for the season. It is Veneno's revenge."

Teresa smiled. "Is that all? Now you can stay here longer."

He stared at her. She shrugged her shoulders and put her hand on his chest.

"Or are you so anxious to leave me?" Her green eyes were cool.

"What is a matador without contracts?" he said bitterly. "One season goes by and he's forgotten."

"You'll accomplish nothing by rushing off to Madrid. All the dates are filled by now."

"They'll need substitutes for those who are gored. If I'm there, the dates will fall to me."

"There are no *corridas* now. You can wait until after Easter, when the season begins. Don't act like a *peón*. Or is it money?"

He waved. "I have enough money."

"Then stay until the season begins. There's nothing in Madrid for you now. Let your sword-handler return and announce that you will return after the season begins. The public will not forget Manolo so quickly."

He looked at her and he did not have to ask if she would come with him because he knew she would not. Here in this fetid atmosphere of wealth and indolence their relationship had changed subtly and he felt it now for the first time. Yet he felt a certain logic in what she said and an insidious appeal to his pride that he found hard to resist. On the other hand, there was Luis and a knowledge

125

that did not fit into words that told him it would be dangerous to remain away any longer.

"I've already told Luis."

"Manuel, he's a sword-handler."

He did not miss the edge of contempt in her words. Four months ago he had felt hatred at the sight of Francisco humbly holding her horse while she mounted, but today her attitude seemed right. He had forgotten Francisco and all Manuel knew was that he was the first matador of Spain and a duke's daughter was his mistress, might possibly become his wife. His attitude did seem somewhat ridiculous.

Luis seemed bewildered by his change of plans, but he said nothing.

"You tell them I'll be back at Easter. Why don't you stay over the night?"

Luis shook his head and set about unpacking Manuel's gear. After Luis had gone Manuel could not shake off the feeling that he had made a mistake, but when he saw Teresa again, his regrets vanished. She was a more pleasant sight than a bull any time.

She did not come with him at Easter either, and before it happened he had guessed that it would be this way.

"I'll come in about a week," she said coolly. "I'll only be in your way in Madrid."

"It's all right for me to hang around here for five months," he said, "but a week in Madrid is too much for the Duchess."

"Really, Manuel, I told you that I'm not one to follow a *cuadrilla*. I never will be."

"You'd better be there for my first fight," he said, "or you don't have to bother coming at all."

"I'll be there," she said cheerfully. "I'll bring everyone with me to see how brave you are."

"Can they stand the sight of blood?"

Her eyes narrowed. "I'll see you in Madrid. I hope your temper has improved by then."

Madrid wasn't the same. The knowledge that he was not fighting corroded any pleasure he might have felt at his return and not having Teresa with him didn't make his mood any more cheerful. He didn't go to Veneno at once, knowing it to be useless. Five months ago he had felt the city was his; now it was alien again. A few people recognized him, but no crowds gathered quickly. If he hadn't been wearing the big sunglasses even those few might have passed him by. In seven months his face had slipped out of the public mind and there were no posters to remind the fans of him. The thought of what it would be like in a year was frightening.

He could not even go to South America, since he had missed the season there. The prospect of hanging around Madrid for a year, waiting for phone calls announcing the goring of a matador, was a depressing one. He knew the pressure that would come from Teresa and for the first time in his life he doubted his own strength. He did not know if he would be able to resist her lures.

He called the boys together. That was another thing. He had let them down and they would have to quit him if he did not get them some fights. He had a good *cuadrilla* and it would not be so good for him to work with pickups. Luis he would have to keep, but he could not afford the others if he did not get a few quick fights.

They were somber when they gathered and he knew they were already thinking about quitting. No jokes about women, none of the careless banter that never seemed to stop when things were going well and they had more fights than they could handle. He made an attempt to dissipate the gloom.

"You should have come to Monte Carlo with me," he said. "The girls there are dying for real men. Did Luis tell you about them?"

It was useless. They remained morose and made no attempt to carry on the raillery.

"Well, what's the picture?" he asked. "By your faces, I guess it's black."

Several of them nodded. None spoke. It was worse than Manuel had anticipated.

"It can't be as bad as those sad faces of yours. We'll be working soon enough. In this business we don't have to wait long for openings. The bulls provide them regularly."

"Some of the boys can't wait, Manolo." It was Luis and Manuel guessed that he had been chosen spokesman for them.

"I know how it is," he replied. "A woman asks no questions except one. But we are a *cuadrilla* and I would like to keep it as such. You will not pick up more in the cafés now."

"That's all good talk," said one of the picadors, "but we don't know if you're going to fight again."

"Are you crazy, man?"

"There's plenty of talk," the picador said stubbornly.

"Talk? What kind of talk?"

"Just talk, Manolo," Luis put in quickly. "The usual worthless rumors of the cafés."

"Don't kid me, Luis. I know the cafés and their talk and you know it also. This is different. Tell me, man."

Luis looked uncomfortable and glanced around at the others. It was the picador who spoke up.

"They're saying you've lost your nerve," he said bluntly. "It's said that you've got a rich woman and the bulls aren't so appealing any more."

"And you believe it!" His face was savage. He stepped toward them, glaring at the semicircle of faces before him. "You believe I've gone cowardly!"

"It's happened before," the picador said stubbornly. "First, no contracts. Then you stay away when the season begins and you don't show up until after Easter. And the rest all fits. Besides, we've got to see some pesetas, Manolo."

"It's that *puta*," Luis said hotly. "I told them it was she who was starting those rumors, but they're only too anxious to listen. They're just like the fans."

"Who?"

"You know," Luis said.

"Mercedes?"

"The same. She is in the cafés every night and she tells it to anyone who will listen. It's not hard to find customers for that kind of garbage. It started right after I found out from Veneno and it's been spreading. That's all they're talking about in the cafés."

He felt the futility of his rage. It could not convince them. Nothing could convince them except a fight, and that he could not provide. It suddenly seemed hopeless to try, and for a moment he felt he was beaten. Mercedes. A subtle revenge she had chosen for herself. And he had played right into her hands. Mercedes and Veneno between them.

All this time he had been playing the lovesick boy with Teresa and they had been sharpening the knife. Teresa. There was another one to blame. Even as he thought it he felt a yearning for her that hurt. Instead of being with him she was probably with some slickly combed dissipate betraying him. The thought enraged him despite his knowledge that it could not be true. At least, not yet. Women. Wherever he turned he found women. Mercedes, Anna, Teresa. Each had played her part in bringing him to his present state.

Still, the men were waiting. They hadn't walked out on him yet and they were looking to him for a lead. There was still a chance if he acted resolutely. The thought of having to convince them he was not a coward was a bitter one.

"All right," he grated. "Money talks. Give me two weeks to see what I can do."

They looked at one another, hesitating.

"Two weeks is not so long," said the picador. "Don't misunderstand, Manolo. We'd like to stay with you, but we have to think of ourselves."

When they left he hurried over to Veneno's office. He would have to control his anger, he knew, but the rage that was in him longed for expression and he could think of no better target than Veneno. It was almost four years since he had last seen him.

He hadn't changed much. He smiled when he saw Manuel come into the office, his manner oily. It was a plain, bare office with several photographs of bullfights on the walls and the stuffed head of a bull mounted on the wall behind Veneno. He was still squat, not any heavier, and he still wore a conservative dark suit.

"Well, Manolo, so you are back." He did not get up or offer his hand.

"You've had your revenge," Manuel rasped. "Are you enjoying it?"

Veneno spread his hands, as if to show they were clean.

"You're talking of contracts, I see." He shrugged. "I could not convince the promoters that you would be in condition to fulfill contracts this season. They wanted to

129

see you, to be sure that your retirement was just for six months."

"Don't bother to lie to me."

Veneno was still smiling and he said nothing.

"I want some fights," Manuel said.

"Where am I to get them?"

"I'd gladly slit your belly, Veneno. Don't tempt me or I'm likely to do it."

Veneno's face went a deep red but he controlled himself. "If you hear of anything, let me know," he said. "I'll arrange it."

"That bilge is all right for the laborers, Veneno, but not for me. They're saying I've lost my nerve. I've got to get a fight. For nothing, if necessary. Just so long as I have a *corrida* here in Madrid. And quickly. If not, you're finished. I'll get another manager and you can sue me for your percentage. You'll never collect it."

"For nothing, you said?" Veneno asked.

"If necessary, for nothing. I need a *corrida*."

A calculating look came into Veneno's face. He turned toward the window and pretended thought, his back to Manuel. When he turned back he seemed to have come to a decision.

"I have an idea," he said. "I'll make a few calls and see what I can do. I think I can arrange something, so long as you don't want any money."

"That's better," Manuel said. "Then we can get some work for the fairs and substitute assignments."

"First a *corrida* in Madrid," Veneno said. "I'll call you later today or tomorrow." His smile was disarming, placating. "After all, I never quarrel with money. You know me, Manolo."

"I know you, all right."

He stalked out. He'd have something lined up inside of two weeks, Manuel thought. One fight sure, even if it was a month off, would be enough to hold the boys together. And to stop the mouths. If they didn't stop, they'd come to see. The first thing he had to do was to get into condition again. Six months, more, since he had last faced cattle. He didn't have to try himself to know how rusty he was.

Veneno called him late in the afternoon, much to Manuel's surprise.

"Manolo? I've got something lined up."

"I thought there was nothing. It's only three hours."

"What do you say to a benefit?"

"For whom?"

"Tono Gómez."

"He must need it. All right. That sounds like a good setup."

"I already told them it was all right with you, Manolo. A week from Thursday. It's all settled."

"A week from Thursday! That's nine days. I'm not in condition."

"That's the only date. Then the *novilleros* start and the plaza is booked. You want to back out?"

Manuel knew he couldn't do that. It would be all over town before nightfall.

"All right. I guess I can fix myself. Who's on the card?"

"The younger Gómez, Victor."

"What, a *novillero?* You're trying to make me ridiculous! I won't do it."

"He took the *alternativa* two weeks ago. He's a full matador now. He's been doing some sensational work. It's a natural and the plaza will be packed."

"Who's the third sword?"

"None. A *mano a mano* between the two of you. And the older Gómez gets the receipts."

Manuel hung up slowly and stared at the telephone. It was too pat. There was a smell about it that he did not like. He had the feeling that he had been tricked.

Chapter Eighteen

In the quiet hours of the morning when the darkness had not yet broken Manuel discovered that the joy of bullfighting had fled from him. The discovery came stealthily, slipping into his soul like an evil dream and waking him from the restless sleep that had shielded him from this knowledge.

Thursday was here, the Thursday when again he was to go out alone to meet his destiny. He came to full wakefulness only slowly, hugging close the desire to sleep, until at last he faced himself in the darkness. All his life since that first day in Madrid he had chosen, had forced the pace, made the decisions, and sought the conflicts. But he had not chosen this.

He was dry, very dry, and he would have liked to ring for a drink but he felt ashamed to do it. Somehow it had all changed for him, how he could not say. The days when every bull was an opportunity, a step upward toward the moment of satiety that seemed distant by a lifetime, had suddenly vanished, and this was a new day for Manuel Ortega, called Manolo by friends and enemies alike. He would have liked to have those days back again, at least once more, those days of hunger for glory, for money, for women, for all of it that he now had.

The knowledge of how far from himself he was had come slowly, disguised by words like "rusty." He knew he was rusty, out of condition, his timing off, his wrists stiff. But knowing all that he had not been troubled much. They were temporary things, phenomena of the body that his genius could surmount. This was different. This was his genius, the distilled essence of it, and his instincts told him that it had fled.

The suspicion that he had been tricked, vague at first, had grown into a certainty as the days moved inexorably toward the fight. Victor Gómez had made his presence felt in the cafés and made no secret of his intentions. Manuel remembered how the horn had found the older Gómez, thrusting again and again even as he ran across the arena to save him. Remembering, Manuel shuddered.

He welcomed the daylight that seeped through the drawn blinds. Details of the room came into focus and their familiarity relaxed him. Light obscured the truth that had come to him in darkness and he laughed at it, relieved that he could laugh. There never had been a day when he wondered if he could do it and this day was no different from the others. He should have known better than to fight bulls in his mind. The place was the plaza with a sword in his hand. But he was still very dry in the mouth.

He heard the boys come in, Luis first, then the others. They had probably seen the bulls already. He lay abed waiting and soon the knock came at his door. Eight o'clock had come quickly. Eight hours were left.

"Come in," he called. "I'm awake."

Luis came in with a pot of coffee, which he set down on the table beside the bed.

"How do you feel, Manolo?"

"Not bad. How is the day?"

Luis poured coffee into a cup and went to the window. He drew the blinds and brightness came into the room.

"A day for the fiesta," he said. "A little wind, but it's early yet."

"Filth of a wind," said Manuel.

Luis frowned. A couple of the other boys came in and stood around. They looked at Manuel and then at Luis. Manuel cursed them to himself for their doubts. Something had happened to his *cuadrilla,* the lightheartedness had gone out of it. He knew a *cuadrilla* always reflected its matador, but he turned away from the knowledge, not wanting to admit its existence. A gust of wind rattled the slats of the blinds. No one said anything. After a while they went out and left him alone again. He missed the chaffing that was customary the morning of a fight.

He missed Paco. It came upon him when he was alone. This was the time Paco always came in, not saying much, but giving a feeling of confidence, reducing the bulls to their real proportions, not letting them become the monsters imagination could create. His first fight without Paco. Irritated with himself, Manuel got out of bed. Outside it was very bright and the wind was negligible. He knew it would be gone by four o'clock.

At eleven o'clock Elena came in, followed by the

133

cuadrilla. She had their breakfast, all they would eat until after the fight. Eggs fried with sauce, rolls, oranges, coffee. They all ate slowly.

"How are my friends the bulls?" Manuel asked.

"The usual," Luis said carefully. "Bugs with stingers."

"How do they come out?"

"The big one first."

"The big one," Manuel echoed. "And the second?"

"The first is a freight train, Manolo. A slow freight, I'm afraid. But the second looks good. Full size, but he charges well. The horns are straight."

"There'll be a full house," Andrés, a picador said. "This has the town completely loco. I never saw Madrid like this."

"They come to see me get it," Manuel said.

They all looked at him and Luis knocked on wood. The silence became heavy, weighing on them all. Luis made a sign with his hand that Manuel was not supposed to see and they got up one by one and went out.

"Don't let the talk upset you," Luis said. "You have to get used to that when you're on top. You've cut plenty of ears. Don't pay any attention to the mouths."

Manuel stared at Luis. A *peón* was telling him how to behave. Did it show that badly? Luis saw a lot more than he showed. So he had to prove himself to his own *cuadrilla* also. A fine state he had come to. He heard the doorbell ring.

"I don't want to see anyone," he told Luis. "I'm going to rest now."

Luis pulled the blinds shut again, darkening the room, and went out quietly. Manuel lay down on the bed, closing his eyes. He had just finished his coffee but his mouth was dry again. A knock at the door.

"Manuel, it is I."

Teresa. He had forgotten her completely. He sat up and got off the bed quickly.

"Come in, come in."

She had arrived the day before and he had seen her only briefly. Now she came into the darkened room bringing with her an atmosphere alien to the bulls. He smelled her perfume before she reached him. When she slipped her

134

arms lightly around his neck and kissed him softly the perfume surrounded him. He held her a moment longer. This was something he still hungered for. With a wrench he remembered that he was going to walk away from this and go out to the horns.

"I've brought some others," she said carelessly. "They wanted to wish you luck."

Before he could object, she went to the door and ushered them in. He could not hide his distaste. There was a French count and the lush-bodied wife of an industrialist. Two others he did not know came in with them.

"I wanted to see you put on those tight pants," the industrialist's wife said. "How do you get into them?"

His face was sour and his eyes were on Teresa. Her green eyes were cool, slightly mocking.

"You're all sitting together?" He had nothing better to say.

"A box," Teresa said.

"I'm so thrilled," the industrialist's wife said. "We've prepared a big party for tonight, Manolo."

"I hope I don't disappoint you," he said. "Maybe you should have invited the bull this time."

She laughed loudly, thinking it very funny.

"I've got to rest now," he said, eager to be rid of them. He hoped that Teresa would stay. She did.

"Wait for me," she said to the others. She slipped off her wrap. "What is it, Manuel?"

She was so beautiful she made him ache even now.

"Nothing," he said, "nothing. Why did you bring them?"

She shrugged her shoulders. "Have a triumph today, Manuel," she said. "I want to boast tonight."

He frowned. She was wearing a black dress cut deep over the bosom and in the gloomy light her very white skin glowed. He realized that it meant nothing to her. He shook his head as if to clear it.

"I'm going to give you my cape," he said. "Is it all right?"

She hesitated only a moment. "Marvelous," she said.

She picked up her wrap. He wanted her to stay. Having her with him a while longer seemed like a wonderful idea.

135

"Stay a while."

She came to him and kissed him, lightly so as not to spoil her make-up.

"I can't. We have an appointment. Have luck."

She went out quickly and left him staring at the empty doorway. She had the lightheartedness, he thought grimly. She had it, all right, and a lot of other things also. He lay down on the bed again, waiting for the hours to go by. Zaragoza had not been like this. It had never been like this.

A triumph, she had said. His mouth twisted. The duke's daughter commanded and the bootblack obeyed. And if there were no triumph? He stopped that one before he finished it. With a growl he pushed himself off the bed and poured himself some water from a carafe. Five minutes later his mouth was as dry as before.

A little before one o'clock Luis came in and started laying out his suit across a chair. The suit of lights, red and gold, gleamed at him in the darkened room. Outside he heard a band playing far away. Bullfight music. A barber came in to shave him and trim his hair. The lather felt good on his face and he let himself relax with the knowledge that he had nothing to do.

The *cuadrilla* went out to dress, and when the barber had gone he looked down at the scars on his right thigh, remembering how Teresa had grimaced when she saw them. He touched them with his fingertips. She wouldn't touch them. Not ever. He had been flattered then, thinking it was for him that she felt. Now he knew better. They were his and his alone and only he knew what they had cost. She wanted him, but she wanted him perfect, without ugliness, without scars, only in strength.

He heard Luis coming back and he knew the time was short now. Once he was in the suit the time would be upon him and thinking would disappear. To his surprise Paco came in with Luis.

"Paco, you!"

"None other," said the old man gravely.

Luis said nothing. Manuel felt the relief spreading over him, the sense of confidence returning to him at the sight of the browned peasant face and the calm light eyes. Paco

136

studied him, unsmiling, waiting for Manuel to say something.

"So you came back, old one!" Manuel was exultant. It was an omen he could not ignore.

Paco looked at Manuel and then at Luis, standing off to the side. His face remained grave.

"I'm glad there is nothing between us," Manuel said.

"You did not expect me?" Paco asked slowly.

"How could I expect you, old one? But you are welcome, have no fear."

"I thought you asked for me," the old man said stiffly.

Manuel paled. "No, I did not ask for you. Why should I ask for you?"

"I thought it strange myself. Since you did not, then I am sorry I have disturbed you before a *corrida*. Much luck."

He turned to go. Manuel wanted to stop him, to reach out and keep him here. The omen was turning into its opposite and the dread was mounting rapidly with each slow step Paco took toward the door. But the pride, the terrible lashing pride, blocked him. All that was needed was a word, one short word, but he thrust it back savagely, hating himself for wanting to say it.

"What made you think I needed you?" he jeered at the retreating figure. "You thought Manolo would go down on his knees? Thank you for your good wishes, but you had better save them for Gómez. I have no need of them."

He watched the old man go out, unruffled by his anger. The pride had defeated his need. He turned to Luis, who was trying to make himself unnoticed.

"You did this." His voice was a snarl. "You took it upon yourself to humble Manolo. You thought I needed a nurse? You think with the others that Manolo is finished?"

Luis backed away from him. "Before God, Manolo, I meant no harm. He knows the bulls, the old one. Better than me. I wanted to do you a service."

"Get out!"

Luis scuttled out. When he was alone the anger vanished quickly. They all thought it of him, even Luis. Even Paco had been ready to believe it. And he himself, did he

137

believe it? The terror of it was that he did not know. The episode had unnerved him, had shattered the carefully erected calm that he had built up since morning. The whole edifice was now rubble. His mind went inevitably to Zaragoza, when there had been no thought, only impatience.

Going to the door he saw the *cuadrilla* huddled together, talking in low voices. He could not hear them. Luis was doing the talking and the picadors were listening. He could guess what he was saying: "Lean on that iron, you motherless scum. Never mind what Manolo says, you listen to me. Chop them down! You hear me, chop them down! Shove that iron in today. None of those little jabs."

They were going to protect him despite himself. He was an investment to them, a big matador who got big fees. Such jobs were not to be had every day. They'd do it all, except that he had to go out to the horns and they were trying to take the danger out of that, plotting how to destroy the bulls, so that what was meant to be a tragedy would become a butchery.

It was easy for him. All he had to do was to pretend he did not know. You didn't hear it, Manuel. It's nothing to you what they're saying. All you've got to do is walk out on the sand with the cape and with the sword and keep your feet still and your face quiet and let them chop them down. Then the horns will be low and you will be able to go in safely, put the sword in anywhere, and get out of it alive. The thought made him cringe. Not that! In all the hours since he had wakened he had not thought of that. Damn Luis and damn Paco and damn them all!

He went to the window and looked out. The crowds were already beginning to stream toward the plaza and the hawkers were out shouting. Lots of girls. It was just three weeks short of the day four years ago when he had vaulted the *barrera* and started himself toward this day. He was very, very dry.

Chapter Nineteen

They came in for the ceremony of dressing him. It was not a simple act and they always did it with dignity and solemnity, falling into the feeling of tragedy that the bullfight inspires. He wore snug, fitted underwear of cotton to absorb the sweat. It reached his knees, covering his scars. Sitting on the bed he let Luis kneel and put the white stockings on his bare feet. Manuel pulled them up over his knees, tucking the underwear into them. The outer stockings, pink, went over the white ones, snugging in his legs.

Next came the tight pants, the *taleguilla,* gold-embroidered and skin-hugging. Manuel put his feet in one at a time and then let Luis work them up over his legs, tugging, smoothing, straightening. It had to be perfect or it could foul up all his movements. Then he sat and Luis laced the breeches below the knees, drawing them tight. They were tighter than usual, testifying to the weight he had put on. Over his feet Luis slipped the soft-soled heelless slippers. A crimson tie and a crimson sash about his waist finished the job.

The mirror told him he was not the gaunt-faced killer he had been. It told him more. The vanity had fled with the pleasure and he did not like the sight of himself and he turned away from it abruptly. Grimly he sat while Luis attached the artificial pigtail, the vestigial caste mark of a matador, to a lock of his hair, testing it to see if it was secure. Then the brocaded vest and, finally, the heavy, gold-embroidered jacket, held by Luis while Manuel snugged himself into it, feeling its weight and its tightness as something more than physical. He carried it like a burden. Save for the *montera,* the black hat, and the elaborate dress cape of silk, he was dressed for the plaza.

"Leave me for a while," he told them.

They always did at this time and they looked at him somberly because he had told them. The blinds were still drawn and the sun had slipped around behind the house now and the room was quite dark for midday. So it had happened to him, to Manolo. He could not hide from it any longer because time was running out now and he had the habit of facing himself. It was not true that he had never been nervous before a fight because they all were nervous before a fight, some of them before all fights.

It was not the bulls, though it was the horns that formed the focus for his apprehension. They were the same bulls he had killed regularly and pitilessly for three years. But he knew he was not the same man, knew it surely. One straw was left to him and he clung to it: that the training of years would assert itself and the vision of the bulls themselves would restore his perspective and shake him out of his preoccupation with himself. The crowd and the activity could push this other thing, still nameless in his brain, out of his mind and free him for the fight.

The door opened quietly and he whirled in anger because he knew the half hour was not yet up. In the gloom he could not see who it was but when she took her first step into the room he recognized her by her movements. It was Mercedes. She closed the door quickly but quietly.

"Hello, Manolo."

Her voice was hoarse and he knew that she was in a state of near exhilaration. She was wearing a white dress and a light fur wrap. Slowly she came toward him while he stared at her, her movements reminding him of the full, warm body.

"How did you get here?"

She chuckled. "I know this house well. Or have you forgotten? I hear no greetings for an old friend. Better than a friend. What friend would give you what I gave?"

"Get out!" His voice was little more than a whisper.

"I will, in good time. I would not keep you from your rendezvous today. No, this is one assignation that I would not bar to you."

She slipped off the fur piece and tossed it carelessly on the bed. The brown skin of her shoulders and chest was taut and she walked with a full-hipped insulting arrogance that enraged him. He should have thrown her out, but he was held by a desire to know what she had to say. That this was a visit of hate he did not doubt.

"You are very quiet this day, Manolo. Has something happened to make you this way?"

"Say your piece, woman, and leave me. I've already thrown you out once. My conversation today is reserved for such as have more honor than you."

"And they will have something to say to you also," she hissed, leaning forward. "Remember, I told you that you would know the day you were to die."

He tried to laugh but the sound strangled in his throat. He watched her tensely, his imagination aiding her in the job she was doing, unable to prevent it.

"Are you seeing them, Manolo? I know you well, better than the duke's daughter knows you, better than yourself. I it was who found you and I it is who am destroying you. None other!"

"Save it for the cafés." The attempted jeer sounded hollow and weak.

She thrust her plain wide face close to his and in the gloom he could see her eyes glittering. There was wine on her breath, which was rapid.

"Can you feel it, Manolo? Can you see it? Can you see the horn reaching for you, thrusting at you, finding you? It is today, Manolo, today, and we all will be there to see it. That is why they come—to see Manolo die. Die!" She paused, glaring at him. "The bull has no pity and neither have I. My hate and your arrogance will kill you this day. What do you say, Manolo?"

"Get out!" His voice was hoarse, rasping, trembling. "Get out!"

He pushed her toward the door and she laughed shrilly. "Today, today!" she repeated, near hysteria.

He pushed her bodily through the door and slammed it shut, leaning against it to make sure she did not somehow return. His mind tried to be cool about it, to tell him that it had been done to unnerve him, but it was no use. His already taut nerves could not stand this added strain and he trembled as he leaned against the door, feeling weak. Death was in his mind, spreading out to take possession of all of him, and he was helpless against it.

Luis came in without knocking but Manuel was not in a state for anger.

"I thought I heard voices from here," Luis said.

Manuel shook his head weakly, not trusting his voice. Luis shrugged and looked puzzled.

"It's time," he said.

"Get me some water," Manuel said.

He rinsed his mouth and then took a last look in the mirror. He knew the word now: fear. He despised himself for it, shame hurting him. But he could not get death out of his mind and in the mirror he saw himself and saw also the bulls. Where had it started? Luis put his cap on his head and picked up a sword case and put it under his arm.

"All right, Manolo?"

Manuel put on the *montera* and took the dress cape and walked out of the darkened room surrounded by his *cuadrilla*. His step was firm and his face composed and none seeing him could guess that this was a man who thought he was going to his death, who, in fact, had been told this a few minutes earlier. There was a small crowd in front of the house and when Manuel stepped out some of them said, *"Olé!"* Dark-faced, he paid no attention, staring straight ahead of him. The sky was totally clear and his suit glittered in the bright sunlight. A boy was rubbing the front fender of the station wagon with a dirty cloth and Luis gave him some coins. The baskets with the capes and muletas were already stowed in the back and Manuel took his accustomed seat in the back in the middle. Surrounded by his men, pressed tightly because of the bulky suits, he was as ready as he would ever be.

"The wind is gone," a *banderillero* said.

"A great day for the fiesta," said another.

They made slow time although the distance was short because the street leading to the plaza was crowded, not only with vehicles, but with people walking in the street. The noise and the movement communicated tension to Manuel who stared straight ahead, alone with himself. This ride was always something he did not like because there was nothing to do except wait and even when he was good he did not like the waiting.

When he got out at the horse gate Manuel could see all the women in the crowd, their clothes gay and bright, their voices strangely moving to him. It was as if he heard in them the goodness of life.

142

All together in a group they moved down the *cuadrilla* passageway under the stands, where it was cool. They saw Gómez' *cuadrilla* up ahead of them and as they drew close one of them said loudly, "Here comes the big shot."

Manuel recognized the man who had been standing by the infirmary when Tono Gómez had been gored.

"They make anybody a matador these days," Luis said just as loudly. "Next week we'll have to fight another benefit."

The *cuadrilla* went out to the arena to deposit the capes, swords, and water bottles, while Manuel stayed under the stands. Victor Gómez came out and grinned coldly at him. Manuel did not return the grin, staring at him with malevolence. Through the opening to the arena he could see the crowd jamming into the stands. Photographers came in and asked Manuel to pose with Victor, but he refused irritably. He offered Victor use of the chapel first and Victor went in.

Then it was his turn and Manuel went in. Always he had said a short prayer, kneeling, doing it right but not believing in it. He could not change today. It had not been prayers that had made him great and it would not be prayers that would keep him alive. He did not pray more than usual, but remained on his knees before the shrine for a while looking for calmness in the dim surroundings with the candles burning on either side of the image of the Virgin. In here there was no noise and he welcomed the silence. He stayed until he felt the dryness in his throat again. I'm afraid, he thought simply.

When he came out he took pains not to show it. The *toreros* were all in place now for the parade into the ring and soon fifty thousand people would fix their eyes on him, Manolo, and while his pride was a bitter thing to him now, it was still there. He set the hat firmly, tossed the dress cape over his left shoulder, and gathered the rest of it at his waist. He stood at the head of his *peones,* head erect, eyes somber. His body gave the impression of arrogance still, though he did not feel it.

Abruptly drumbeats shattered the air, followed immediately by an immense shout from beyond the gate, which swung out. Manuel straightened, lifting his head. The music began and he heard the trumpet sounding—

143

sounding for him. Then he stepped out in time to the music, unconsciously realizing that Victor Gómez, hate or no hate, had deferred to him. The parade moved into the sunlight as the ovation swelled. Manuel did not look at the stands, but fixed his eyes on the president's box and marched toward it, bowing slightly when he was before it.

In the passageway he quickly found where Teresa was sitting and slipped off the silk cape and gave it to Luis, who took it to her. There was a murmur from the crowd as she spread it wide on the railing before her. Manuel felt his distaste grow at the sight of her friends. Then he saw Victor Gómez' cape being spread, off to the right a bit, and Mercedes was there. Veneno also.

Now he knew it all.

They had not left much to chance. The panic welled up at the thought and he turned away abruptly, rage and fear mingled in him. The bulls, they depended on the bulls. His eyes were pulled toward the door from which they would come and his body seemed to lose all sentience. To break the feeling he picked up a water jug and rinsed his mouth, giving himself something to do. He spat it out on the sand, watching Luis wetting the ends of the capes and scuffing them in the sand with his shoe.

Paco was there also. They had gathered to see the end, Manuel thought. All the vultures. Perhaps the foreign girl, Anna, had also come. He searched for her but could not find her. She had her own bulls to meet. He took his place behind a *burladero,* waiting now for the trumpet. He saw Enrique and Chepe take their places, ready to run the bull. The big one, the freight train.

So it had not vanished by itself. That was what he was thinking. What had vanished, instead, was his bravery. He had pride still, but he was without valor. Well, the pride would have to suffice this day, the pride and the memory of his body. He looked over at Victor Gómez and saw the other matador watching him, stolid-faced, the eyes unreadable. He did not look at Teresa.

The trumpet sounded and the *alguacíl* galloped across the ring on his stiff-legged mount and tossed the key down to a servant, who swung open the door, and Manuel Ortega felt all of him reach out toward that dark emptiness

144

that the door disclosed. He, Manuel Ortega, one of the disinherited of this earth, waited to see his fate come rushing out of the darkness. The sunlit distance between him and the door was vast and arid.

Chapter Twenty

As senior matador Manuel had the first bull. He was big, all right, big, gray, and wide-horned. The pink and green *divisa* ribbons fluttered from his shoulder in the sunlight and a roar rose from the throng at the sight of him. There was no calmness in Manuel as he watched the bull, Rosario, Number 37, rush across the ring toward the *peón* Chepe, who waved his cape and dodged behind a *burladero*. The horns lashed at the planks.

Immediately from the opposite side of the arena Enrique ran out with his cape and the bull whirled and charged toward him. Enrique easily slipped behind the planks a step ahead of the bull. Again the bull hooked at the shield and splinters flew from it.

"He sees well," Luis said.

"Lots of bull," Manuel muttered. "A freight train is right. Run him, Luis."

He watched Luis go out quickly, halting about ten yards from the *barrera,* holding the cape in front of him. Luis did not have to stand still or be graceful, since he was not a matador and his job was only to pass the bull so that Manuel could judge him and see which horn he favored in hooking. The bull rushed and Luis swung the cape out wide and stepped aside, avoiding the charge. The bull checked his charge, braking with his feet, and rushed again, and Luis took him from the other side. Luis ducked behind the *burladero.*

"He favors the left," Luis said.

"Run him again."

Luis shrugged his shoulders and went out a second time. The crowd was quiet, waiting. Luis looked around at the terrain and when the bull started for him he ran at an angle toward one of the *burladeros,* dragging the cape along the ground, zigzagging in front of the bull, which hooked at the elusive cloth. Luis timed his run well and slipped behind the shield a moment before the bull's horns slammed against the wood. Breathing hard, Luis looked at Manuel. The bull, also out of breath, turned away from the timbers.

Manuel went out toward his enemy. As though from far away he heard the crowd cheer as he stepped slowly away from the *barrera* with his cape. The arrogant carriage and the dark grim face served well to hide his unsteadiness. His grip on the scarlet cape was very tight. He backed away from the bull, which had seen him, and then stepped toward it, covering his body with the cape. His right wrist made a small, precise movement, which started the lower far end of the cape swinging gently, catching the bull's eye.

It came at him and he was thinking the words "freight train" as it came, and as the horns lowered his arms went out from his body and the cape spread wide and flicked upward as Manuel stepped back from the hurtling gray bulk. The stands were silent. He pivoted, again facing the bull, holding the cape low. The left horn this time. He did the same thing again, wrists, arms, cape, everything doing the right things, the bull following, the wide horns dropping to hook—and then his feet skittered backward and his arms sent the cape high. A wide space of daylight showed between him and the bull. The stands were silent again.

Manuel was sweating now and panic was beginning to build up in him. He had to control it, to crush the terrible flare of fear that had jerked his feet. The bull returned, charging again, and Manuel again pulled away from the horns at the last moment. The stands were not silent now and he could hear the first shrill jeers. The sound made him cringe. He forced himself to face the bull, provoking another charge, and wrenched the bull savagely, then walked away. It was nothing, no art, no bravery, just revenge on a brave animal. The jeering continued, louder now. He walked to the *barrera,* letting Chepe control the bull. Andrés came in on his horse and Luis said something to him that Manuel could not hear.

Manuel came out again with the cape, setting himself between the bull and the horse, and he guided the bull into the charge. Andrés, braced for the shock, shot the iron point into the left shoulder, ignoring the hump of muscle. The lance ripped a wide gash and Andrés leaned on it and the bull continued thrusting with his horns, looking for the horse, finding the padding, lifting with the great neck muscles, the horse falling and the bull still hooking. Capes were flapping now and the bull left the horse to charge the capes, while a *mono* picked Andrés up. The crowd was shouting its protest against the use of the lance to cripple the bull.

This was the first *quite* and it was Manuel's to do. He could redeem himself now with a series of passes with the cape. But he came out automatically, his mind not on the bull but on himself, obsessed with the fear he had shown, unable to break out of the pattern he had suddenly fallen into. The bull charged his cape, but he passed him like a *peón,* leaping aside from the charge. The second picador was ready for the next charge, and as the gray bull slammed into the horse Manuel heard the crowd again hooting, whistling, shouting curses.

Shaken, he leaned against the *barrera,* watching the confused scene. Again the lance went into the left shoulder. They were trying to ruin the bull, to take all danger out of him, to make his better horn worthless. The picador held the iron in the wound, twisting it, while blood pumped out heavily. With a glance at Manuel, Victor Gómez went out to the bull, slowly, his head high. He stamped both feet down hard on the ground for the whole crowd to see and Manuel went sick with shame.

Victor Gómez took the bull out from the horse with a whirling cape, holding his ground, passing the bull with a series of veronicas that made Manuel's look like the work of a frightened apprentice. Manuel heard the loud *Olé* and that hurt more than all the rest. Grim-faced, he watched Gómez, trying to estimate him, but his mind was not on it. He, Manolo, had shown fear in the bull ring. The trumpet blew and the horses left the ring.

"Are you going to place the *banderillas?*" Luis asked.
Manuel shook his head. "You do it," he said tightly.
Luis nodded.

Victor Gómez was leaning against the *barrera* about ten paces away, his eyes on Manuel. Manuel saw his wide face, hard, hating. When he looked at him Victor gave him a vicious smile. Manuel did not turn to face the stands. He was afraid to look at where Teresa sat.

Too quickly the trumpet sounded again and now was the last little time he had before he must take the sword

148

and go out to the horns alone. Despite all the punishment the bull had taken, the horns were still wide, high, and pointed.

Luis had placed the *banderillas,* hooking the long shafts into the hump of muscle at the bull's neck as it charged and now he handed Manuel the muleta and Manuel stepped out of the *burladero.* Luis held out a sword handle, wrapped in red flannel, and Manuel pulled it from the leather scabbard over the planks. Sword and muleta in his left hand, he went stiff-legged before the president's box, doffing the black *montera,* bowing slightly, asking, as he had so many times, the routine permission to kill. Blank-faced, the president nodded.

He handed the hat to Luis, seeing his somber, worried face, and turned and walked out to the horns with the muleta in his left hand and the sword in his right. He hated each step that took him toward the bull, hated the death that he despised himself for fearing. He saw the blood and the dust on the bull, saw that it was tired, tired of chasing a cloth and wanted a man to hook instead. The crowd was silent, not sure that he was afraid.

It was not the way it had been in Zaragoza, when death had sat on his arm and gone out to the bull, when there had been no other possibility in his mind. The world had lain at his feet then, a sword's length away, and he had gone out to seize it, to claim it as his own. Death sat on the horn now and was reaching out for him. And he knew it.

Not for nothing had Manuel Ortega, called Manolo, been the best. Not for nothing had he the genius in his wrists to dominate the horns in front of him. He used it now to cheat death, unfurling the scarlet muleta, leading the horns away from him, keeping space between him and them, working on the monster in front of him, wrenching the neck from side to side, chopping the cloth back and forth, leading the bull from side to side, never letting it get a full charge, holding it at arm's length, deaf now to the cheers and the shouts and the whistles, hearing only the terrifying clamor of his own fear.

He held death at bay. It was not a performance, it had nothing of beauty and drama in it. It had only the ugliness of naked fear and the desperation of a pitiless struggle for

149

survival. All dignity was gone. There was the blood of the bull and his heat, there were the horns thirsting for him and there was the red cloth, dominating the bull's vision, misusing its strength, dissipating its life as the red blood pumped out while Manuel waited for its weakness to be such that danger would be gone.

But he too tired and the wrist grew weary, the eyes grew blurred with sweat dripping into them, and in one anguished moment the bull got too close. It missed with the horns but bumped with the shoulder and threw him to the ground. Manuel heard the whuff of the bull's breath, felt its nose bump him while he kicked with his feet at the wet muzzle. It was now. A red cape flopped over the bull's face and a pair of hands dragged Manuel clear. Luis.

"He's tired now, Manolo," Luis said in his ear, wiping Manuel's face with a towel. "He's learning fast. Finish it now."

Manuel stared at him and then turned away, looking up at the stands. The fans were standing, screaming down at him. They could not reach him now with their insults. He was beyond caring for that. He knew only that it was his life that was threatened out there, that it was his body that was the target, that there was no pride and no shame if there was no life. He went out slowly. He hated the bull as he had never hated before, but the hate did not arm him against this fear. Instead it made him resolute in it.

He chopped the bull into position with a few passes with the cloth, seeing the forefeet pull together. Now. He ran at the bull from an angle, holding the sword high. Even as he ran the crowd began to scream "Coward!" at him, but he continued, running across the angle of the bull's charge, guiding it past him with the cloth, avoiding the horns entirely, and thrusting with the sword at arm's length, finding the bull's neck and pushing it in. The bull stopped, swayed, hemorrhaged from the mouth, and toppled slowly. Head bowed, Manuel stared at his dying enemy. He turned and walked slowly toward the *barrera*. Cushions flew from the stands, skidding in the sand at his feet, throwing puffs of dust over him.

He did not care. He was alive and the bull was dead. One more and he could leave the arena. His teeth bared, he faced the howling stands, absorbing their insults.

150

"Give me a drink," he said to Luis.

He filled his mouth with water and squirted it in the direction of the stands. A bottle sailed out and clattered against the planks and guards closed around him protectively. Guards protecting him. He shook his head. Carefully he glanced up. Teresa was still there. The shame twisted in him, hurting. He heard the clank of the chains behind him as they dragged the brave bull's carcass from the arena. Victor Gómez took his position in a *burladero*, his face composed. Now would come the worst.

Gómez' bull was smaller than his, all black, with a glossy coat and a long tassled tail. A handsome animal with horns that were straight and not too long.

"He's got a good one there," Luis said.

Manuel said nothing. He watched. Gómez did nothing sensational, a series of passable veronicas, nothing more. The contrast with Manuel, however, won him applause. The applause hurt.

"That's the *fenómeno?*" said Luis.

Manuel remained silent. Gómez guided the bull into the first horse and Manuel went out into the ring with his cape, waiting. Gómez picked up the bull when it left the picador and guided it away, using the butterfly pass, the cape behind him, the ends flicking out on either side, zigzagging the bull across the arena. The *Olé* from the stands was sharp and crackling.

"He gave himself plenty of room," Luis muttered.

Manuel came out after the next horse, the dread not so great this time. Perhaps it was that the bull was smaller or that he had gone through the first ordeal without damage. He tried nothing much, keeping safe distance between him and the bull, but he managed to control his feet this time. The jeers were not so bad.

"He's showing me up," he said when he went back.

This time it was Luis who said nothing.

Gómez worked well with the bull, building up his performance carefully, progressing with each series of passes to more difficult ones. He placed his own *banderillas*, not too gracefully—he did not have the figure for it—but well. He got an ovation for his work. When he came out with the sword he bowed deeply.

"I dedicate this bull to my brother, Tono Gómez, who

151

gave his all before the most discerning public in the world."

Manuel felt the barb in that, recognized Mercedes' touch. It was their day. Leaning on the planks, he watched Gómez go out to the bull, unfurling the muleta. The sun was on his suit of green and gold and he had gained confidence from Manuel's failure, causing him to walk with an arrogance that was not normally his. The sun glinted on the bared sword. He began with the *pase de la muerte*, the pass of death, pulling the horns past his chest.

His *faena* was a good one with a varied repertoire. He passed the bull ten times, pivoting in a yard circle, using both left- and right-handed passes, concluding with a tight pass that turned the bull short and left him fixed in place. As the *Olé* swelled over the plaza Gómez reached over and calmly patted the bull's muzzle.

"Cheap stuff," growled Luis.

Manuel said nothing, staring at the scene impassively.

"Playing up to the sunny-side rabble," Luis continued.

"He'll get his ear," said Manuel.

"If he can kill. Let's see how he is with the hatpin, this *fenómeno*."

The stands were on their feet, cheering.

"That's how it's done, Killer!" someone called.

Manuel did not turn. His face was grim.

But Gómez was not finished. He took the bull out to the center of the arena and started a new series of passes more difficult and tricky. With each pass the *Olés* grew louder. Manuel heard them close to him, feeling each one deep inside himself. They all hurt. Luis continued his running comment on Gómez' performance and Manuel knew that it was true, that Gómez looked good only because he himself had been so bad.

The time for the killing had come. Gómez faced the bull and then launched himself on the animal quickly, too quickly. The sword went in and Gómez stood over the animal, watching it fall. The stands were in an uproar. He leaned over, back to the stands, and pulled the sword out, wiping it on the muleta. Then he turned and bowed. The band struck up. One of his *cuadrilla* ran up and sliced off the bull's ear with a short knife and ran toward the president's box, holding it aloft. The clamor in the stands con tinued and they forced Gómez to make a tour of the ring. The president nodded and the *peón* ran to Gómez and thrust the bloody ear into his hand. Gómez held it up for the crowd to see, grinning happily.

He came back to where Manuel was standing and stopped. He held the ear in his palm and let Manuel see it. Manuel did not move.

"A comedian," growled Luis.

Manuel was beyond it. The time was now. He watched the dead bull being dragged from the ring and the *monos* come out to smooth the sand. The cheers had belonged to him before, but now they belonged to Victor Gómez. His eyes were on the gate from which the next bull would come. Once today he had cheated death. Now he would be able to do so no longer. Gómez' ovation was still continuing, but he no longer heard it. Closer to him, enveloping him, was the pulse of his own life, warm, precious, frantic. He felt nothing but the knowledge that the time had come, that the cheers were meant to thrust him into it, to fence him in and give him no escape. Brooding, alone, he waited for the trumpet. It was to be here on the gray-tan sand of the Madrid arena under a high and cloudless sky of blue that the end of the quest would come.

Chapter Twenty-One

The first glance told him that his second bull was perfect.
Not too small like Gómez', not big and slow like his first,
but a full-grown animal, quicker than a polo pony, with
full-sized horns that curved forward gracefully. On
another day this animal would have been all he could ask.
He watched the *peones* take him through the preliminary
passes.

When he stepped out with his cape the crowd set up a
clamor against him. They did not want to be cheated with
this bull by a coward who was too afraid of the bull to
dominate him. Deaf to them, Manuel took his position,
waving out the cape. The bull shot straight for him. His
speed sent the panic flooding through Manuel and his feet
jittered away from the charge while his upflung cape sent
the bull dashing clear across the arena. A frenzy of cat-
calls and insults poured down from the stands.

Then, as he waited for the bull to come back, deter-
mined on his course, a shirt-clad figure vaulted the *barrera*
at the far side of the arena and came running crookedly
toward the bull. The hisses turned to loud cheers at the
sight of the amateur running to meet the bull. The anger
that caught Manuel made him tremble.

The youth flashed in front of the bull waving a
homemade cape. The bull charged and the youth held his
position awkwardly, waving the cape in front of the horns.

"Get that amateur," Manuel grated to Luis. "Get that
damned lousy punk out. If the horns don't rip him up, I
will."

The *peones* were out with their capes and the *monos*
were running after the amateur, who was dodging and running around the arena, drawing laughter and good-natured
cheers. The bull-ring servants finally collared him and
pushed him toward a *burladero*. Manuel saw the youth,
saw his lean face, flushed now with exertion, saw the rough
grip they held him in. Feeling fell away from Manuel as he
watched the scene and time fell away.

In the passageway the guards grabbed him, one twisting his arm up behind his back. Manuel watched, ignoring

the bull. As he watched a bright red flower fluttered down from the stands, landing at the youth's feet. He twisted out of the guards' hands, bent, and picked up the rose. Then he was gone, hustled under the stands by the guards.

The red, red flower stayed in Manuel's mind. He did not hear the cruel taunts of the crowd and he did not face the bull. He was looking backward, looking deep into himself. Then feeling returned and with it came pain, pain so great that it could not be borne. His lips pulled back from his teeth and he felt the pain twisting in him, pushing deeper, reaching the very bottom of his soul, where the shame and the fear were.

He looked up at the stands, seeing them but not hearing them. Teresa was gone. He saw the empty space behind the cape and the pain lurched inside him. It was something he had always known but that did not stop the hurting. He could imagine how her face had lifted with disdain, how her mouth had gone cruel, how one short phrase had come out of the cruel red mouth, and how she had risen, followed by the others, and gone out of his life forever.

He saw Mercedes, saw her smiling, saw Veneno smiling.

"Better and better," she was saying.

"He deserved it," Veneno was answering. "I would not have missed it for anything."

"There is more yet," Mercedes was continuing. "There is yet the final act, the attempt to salvage honor from shame."

"It will be a disaster."

"His disaster, my triumph."

"I forgive you everything for this."

Manuel saw them. He saw all of them who were waiting for his blood. They demanded the final test of his manhood. This was where the quest led. Matadors begin and matadors finish, but the bulls go on forever. In each man's life there is a horn and it cannot be evaded. He knew it now and beside this knowledge all else faded away. He turned back to the arena.

The horses were on the sand now and he strode out to the bull.

"Save this animal," he warned Luis. "Do not spoil him."

He shook out the cape and the bull catapulted toward him, past him, shooting at the horse. The lance dug into the crest of muscle and the horns found the padding, threw horse and rider. Still hooking, the horns found the horse's chest, hooked once, twice, and the horse was dead. Capes flopped wildly while *monos* reached frantically for Andrés, the picador, lying under the horse.

Manuel's cape took the bull away. He showed them a *mariposa,* a butterfly pass that was graceful, arrogant, unhurried, the cape behind him, the ends flicking the bull's ears, first one and then the other, as he paced backwards across the arena, the bull following as though hypnotized by the gently fluttering ends of the cape, never once hooking at his exposed body. He finished the *quite* with a *serpentina,* twisting the cape out with a snaking flourish that spun the bull dizzily. He walked away from it with the *Olé* roaring in his heart.

It had not come that time. Death rode the horn, but it had patience and would draw the last act out. He faced it calmly now. They in the stands, who had cheered him and insulted him, who had made him and who now wanted to finish him, would have to wait for death to make its move. Manuel was finished with running. What he did now, he did not do for them. He did it for himself.

Here was his goal reached at last. In the final hour of his life he had found it, knew it for truth. All his life he had done for others, acted to prove himself in the eyes of others. It had been futile. What mattered was how he looked to himself. He had done all a man could do to prove himself to the world, but when it came time to turn his back on it, it had happened overnight. Only his own soul would admit no such trickery, and knowing this, knowing it, without pretense and without arrogance, he felt shame slip away, gone forever, and the stripped-bare cleanness of it was as sweet and perfect as a feeling could ever be.

Victor Gómez responded to the goad. Somber-faced, he strode out for his *quite,* striving to maintain his triumph. Manuel, intent, saw it happen, saw him underestimate the bull's speed, saw the cape linger too long in front of the body, and saw the horns scoop low and saw Gómez flung upward. He heard the hissing rip of silk, and, as he was running across the sand, saw the blood show on Gómez' leg. He kicked his foot into the bull's muzzle, shoved the cape in front of it, and led it away, a step at a time, while Gómez was lifted and rushed off to the infirmary.

It was all his now. He took the bull with its wet horn out to the center of the arena and stamped both feet down hard, nailing them for all to see. Here he took his stand. The cape swirled out rosily. He passed the bull in a series of veronicas, holding the cape low so that it dragged on the ground, moving it so slowly that the bull seemed to walk by him, its nose glued to the cloth. Man and beast were one, moving in a savagely graceful dance, with death the ultimate partner for one.

It was not that time, either. He walked away with the crowd thundering its emotion at him, but he was as far from their cheers now as he had been from their jeers.

"Boss, I'm ten years older," Luis croaked, wide-eyed.

Unsmiling, Manuel looked at Luis and then up at the stands. He saw Veneno glum and Mercedes staring at him. She was still waiting.

"Nail the sticks," he told Luis. "I have two bulls left."

The crowd was bored with the *banderillero,* wanting Manolo again. He stood behind the planks with his back to them, staring out at the arena, letting the time run out swiftly. It was hard for him not to feel a sadness at this time. Because he was truly alone now, more than ever in his life, and it would have been good to have at least one person to whom it was important. He had not lived that way, and how you lived decided how you died. The sound of the trumpet was clear and defiant, without any mournfulness in it.

When a man goes out to face death, his death, then it is that what he is will show itself. Manuel's horn, the one set aside for him, beckoned, and he strode out to face it. The head was held with the same arrogance, and the face had the same wolflike ferocity it always wore when he went out with the sword.

But inside he was stripped. There was no room for vanity in him now or the false arrogance of those who are ignorant of their fate. He went out to combat knowing that this was the time. Once again the bull was not his enemy but his destiny, but this time he knew it starkly, without adornment.

157

The crowd fell quiet suddenly, the mood of tragedy somehow communicating itself to them. Manuel walked out to the bull and took his stand, lithe, thin-hipped, a gaunt figure in red and gold. The scarlet muleta was furled over the notched stick in his left hand, the sword held loosely in his right.

"*Toro!*" he called crisply. "*Toro!*"

He saw the barbed sticks hanging down along the bull's shoulders and he saw the blood mingled with the sand of the arena, glossing the black hide redly. He saw the small eyes focus on him and he saw the wet horn. Quietly, only his wrist moving, he flicked the scarlet cloth, dropped it to his feet. The bull launched itself and only Manuel's left arm moved as he called death to himself, lifting the cloth slowly, passing the horn past his belly, two inches away. Blood from the bull wiped off on his suit. The *Olé* from the spectators was sudden, explosive, as though they had held their breath and let it out in unison.

Again he called death to him with the red cloth, holding it true to its path with the slow arrogance of his movements, pulling the sharp horns past him, fixed in the scarlet cloth, turning with each charge, flicking the cloth away as the horns passed to hold the bull close, keeping him close, leering at death, pass after pass with a slowness that wrenched shout after shout from the crowd.

When he pulled the beast around himself so tightly that it could not turn, he walked away from it, his back to the horns. The plaza was on its feet, near hysteria. He gave the bull time to recover and then went out to it again, walking solemnly out, drawing a circle with the end of the notched stick and standing within it, telling them all that here in this spot he had chosen he would wait for death to come, not moving from it.

He raised his head in the air, fixed his eyes on the bright blueness of the sky, and raised the red cloth, calling, "*Toro!*" as the stands fell silent. Unseeing, he called the horns to him, standing in the circle, pivoting with each charge, hearing the beast's grunt, feeling its heat. The scarlet cloth traced its line and the bull followed it, its horns held to the belly with the warm life inside it.

Now Manuel saw it all, the horns and death, and he

would not flinch from it. It was a coldness to freeze the heat in him and a dryness to wither the rich life in him and a vastness to swallow up his loneliness. He felt the magnificence of life and knew death to be but a small part of it and he could face it unafraid. The red and the gold and the black were all one in the sinuous whirling movements that caught the crowd by the throat and squeezed out the last drop of its fear.

Because the fear had gone into the vast arena, brought death close to all who watched the elemental struggle on the sands below, made it a part of them, intense and menacing. They felt the violence of the beast, felt the threat in its darkness and its strength, and they clutched at life with one voice, hugging it close, seeing it identified with the slim figure far below them.

The bull caught Manuel at the end of the series of passes. It turned in on him by a fraction of an inch and its bulk hurled him to the ground. Whirling, it was upon him, digging with the horn, chopping, hooking, its hot breath wetting him. He fought for his life. He fought until the capes should reach him, kicking at the brutal snout, pushing the notched stick into it, blinding it with the red cloth as he lay on the ground.

When he was pulled to his feet, the jacket was torn and he was covered with blood. But he was unhurt. The horns had missed. The blood was the bull's. Wordlessly he reached for his sword and cloth and went out again. He took the bull in its own terrain, heedless of death, scorning it, asking for it to come to him as he was going to the bull. Then, when he felt the strength go out of the bull, he turned his back on it and walked away, hearing the tumult from the stands, but far from it.

This was all. One would live and one would die. He knew it now with serenity. His manhood was not something he had to hold up before the world, to do braggart deeds to prove. With the torn jacket and the bull's blood on him, with the scarlet cloth and the naked steel of the sword he went out, his pride no longer something to be flaunted, but to be treasured, to be held as dear as the life he risked.

The quest that had begun on these same sands in the long years back before he was a man had now come to an end. He had found what he had sought—himself. He was a man and he knew it truly, with pride and with humility.

The scarlet cloth furled, he faced the bull. The bull watched him with small red eyes, at bay, wanting to wet its horn once more. Softly, in a voice intimate between himself and the bull, he called to it. Now it was death's time.

He came in slowly, step by proud step, holding the sword up, moving toward the horns that waited for him, crossing the left hand slowly, dragging the moment out with perilous grace, mounting over the horns, feeling the shock as the bull lifted to meet him, feeling the sword penetrate, and standing, drained, seeing the bull begin to topple, knowing death had once more sat on his arm and passed away from him.

The noise broke over him like a thunderclap, but he kept his back to them, staring down at the bull. He pulled out the sword and held it for a moment and then passed it to his left hand. Bending, he leaned over and patted the dead bull softly between the eyes. When he turned to face the ovation, the wolflike quality was gone from his face. He saw a rose flutter from the stands and fall to the sand.